Vengeance

Resslar University Mysteries
Book 2

Vengeance

Resslar University Mysteries
Book 2

Allegra Craver

To my friends, at home and school, who remind me to look on the bright side even in the darkest of times.

**Vengeance: Resslar University Mysteries
Book 2**

Copyright © 2021 Allegra Craver

Content Editor: Darla Billington
Copy Editor: Saeide Mirzaei
Cover Design: Cooper Schwartz
Editor-in-Chief: Kristi King-Morgan
Formatting: Kristi King-Morgan
Assistant Editor: Amanda Clarke

ISBN- 978-1-947381-47-6

www.dreamingbigpublications.com

Acknowledgements

When the image of a girl sitting in her college library investigating an underground fraternity popped into my head freshman year, I never thought it would take me this far. Though many ideas have come and gone, *Vengeance* and *Unraveling* are the first two novels I ever finished in their entirety. I'm immensely proud, but it wouldn't have been possible without the wonderful people in my life.

To my family. You guys are my greatest treasure and loudest cheerleaders. I couldn't be more grateful for your constant humor, love, and support. I love you all so so so much. Thank you for everything.

To my mischievous foster-kitty-turned-cat-daughter Nala. I appreciate your calming nature, despite you doing everything at an 11. Thank you for being a lovely companion through thick and thin.

To my friends for reminding me who I am and what I love. Even if you don't think your antics make it into novels, they do, trust me. Thank you for watching bad movies and shows with me so I could see what not to do. Laughing with you all is one of my greatest joys.

To my classmates and fellow students at Syracuse University. Walking around campus each day was an endless inspirational adventure. Thank you to my professors, my roommates, and my confidants for helping me make sense of my ideas.

To the team at Dreaming Big Publications, those who worked on *Unraveling* and this novel. Your expertise, guidance, and open-mindedness brought my novels to life. You helped fulfill a childhood dream of mine and I'll be forever appreciative of your time and dedication.

To the characters in my head who helped me through my college years–Brooklyn, Nate, Drew, Kennedy, Finn, Taylor, Ryker, and the rest of them. I have written countless essays and exams, have faced challenges greater than myself, have experienced failure and joy, and you all were there right beside me. I'll always listen and if there's another story I have to tell, I will. For now, it's a bittersweet goodbye.

And to you, Reader, for indulging in this story and sticking with Brooklyn until the end.

1

It's snowing. I only notice because of the white flakes flying by my face and collecting around my boots on the grass, along with the dust from the house that's being knocked down mere feet away.

I probably shouldn't be standing this close to the demolition site. The Sigma Eta Alpha house could harbor asbestos, lead paint, or some other poison I'm unwittingly breathing in. Half of the house is in rubble on the ground, destroyed by the bulldozer that's driving into the side of the building, reducing the siding and drywall to mere dust. The noise alone is enough to keep people away, but I don't mind it. The grinding of the machinery sounds more like music than anything else.

"Hey!" barks a voice as two hands come down on my shoulders. I involuntarily jump a bit, but when I turn, I see my boyfriend standing behind me, and the momentary shock dissipates. His amber eyes sparkle as he smiles down at me.

"You scared me!" I chide, slapping him playfully on the shoulder. Nate laughs, kisses me on the forehead, and comes to stand beside me.

"I thought nothing could scare you at this point," he says.

"Unless someone sneaks up on me," I admit.

"Very true," he agrees. He admires the house as it's torn down. When another massive sheet of siding hits the ground, it raises a dust cloud, forcing Nate and I to shield our faces.

"Can you believe it's been a year?" I ask Nate after the dust falls.

"No way. It feels like yesterday that I was in that basement," says Nate.

"It *has* gone by pretty fast when I think about it."

"Well, being whisked from interview to interview usually makes time fly by," he says.

"If I'm put under one more studio light, I swear to God," I joke, sounding as though I'll lose my patience. Talking about interviews makes me remember my responsibilities. I quickly whip out my phone from my pocket and check the time. "Shit, it's one o'clock. I have to go show a freshman around WRDW."

"Alright. I need to get home anyway." Nate kisses me on the top of the head. "Bye. Have fun."

"Bye!" I call after him, watching him cross the street to catch the bus. I take one quick look back at the crumbling SHA house and then make my way around the cloud of dust that's blooming out of the ongoing demolition.

As I walk to the radio station, people are pulling on their hoods and shoving their hands in their pockets. The flakes of snow have morphed into sizeable drops hitting the ground and sticking at a rapid pace. It's only

November, but winter always comes early to Central New York. The Resslar University campus seems quaint when it's hidden under a white blanket. I love the snow, but I hate it when snowflakes get stuck in my eyelashes as I briskly walk towards my second home.

The interior of the station is overwhelmingly warm, compared to the temperature outside. I take my hood off and walk directly to the newsroom where I hang up my jacket. The melting snow drips onto the floor. It's so quiet that I can hear each drop hit the carpet. I relish the silence for a second before Laura, a junior, walks up to me like she's the most important person in the world. She flicks a folder in my direction matter-of-factly.

"These are all the stories that need editing. Peter wants them to run tonight," she says. As soon as I take the folder, Laura purses her lips. I glance down at the folder and nod in understanding.

"Alright, I'll look these over," I tell her. Laura turns away in a huff. "Hey, Laura?" She turns back around. "I only wanted the folder, not the attitude." Laura groans, drops her folded arms, and walks away. I roll my eyes and flip through the six stories in the folder. I'll get these done in an hour, easy. It never takes me long to edit news stories. Writing them, though, is a different animal altogether.

"Brooklyn?" says a weary voice from the doorway. I turn to see Peter, the adult manager of the station, watching me with weary eyes from behind his square wire frames. The beige color of his suit blends into the wall behind him, save his dark red tie. He's never actually tired, but he always looks like someone who hasn't slept in a few days. "Have you met your trainee yet?"

"No, Sir. I just got stories from Laura," I say, waving the folder as proof. "I'll show him around. Where is he?"

"Just got in," says Peter as I put the folder down near my backpack and begin to walk out of the door. "Oh, and Brooklyn! Make sure he doesn't–"

"Touch anything he's not supposed to. Got it," I say with a smile, remembering Peter's warning to Ryker, who had shown me around when I had first started working here.

"Exactly. Go on." My boss nods towards the lobby, and I take that as my cue to leave.

Sure enough, sitting in a squishy chair, there's a boy who seems to have appeared out of thin air. He looks innocent enough with a somewhat chiseled face, tawny blonde hair, and light green eyes that are searching the room. Eventually, they rest on me. The boy's mouth curves into a smile, and he stands.

"You must be my trainee," I say, shaking his hand. "Brooklyn Perce, Student Manager of WRDW."

"Conor Valree, manager of nothing," he says, with a little laugh. "Nice to meet you."

"You too. So, you're working as my intern. I don't know if anyone's told you yet, but too bad, you're stuck with me," I joke, leading him out of the lobby area and towards the newsroom. Conor snorts but silently follows me like a shadow.

We enter the newsroom where his translucent eyes search the walls, looking at the accolades the station and its various reporters have won over the years.

"Impressive," he says under his breath.

"Very. So, this is the newsroom. It's pretty big for the nights where there's about twenty people in here for elections, midterms, big football games, things like that. These little editing suites are where you'll write your story, edit sound, the whole nine yards." I walk through the newsroom and wave hello to Laura who's sitting in a suite and only rolls her eyes back in response.

"Is she always this friendly?" asks Conor as we leave.

"Laura's a charmer," I say sarcastically. "And she's not at all bitter that I became manager over her." I open the door to the stairwell for him. "So, you interviewed with Peter earlier this week?"

"Yeah, I did," he answers as he climbs the stairs behind me. "Seems nice enough. Didn't mention I'd be *your* intern, though." I pause at the landing, my hand on the doorknob to the top floor of the building.

"Why am I so special?" I ask, stifling a groan.

"C'mon, Brooklyn. I want to be a journalist. I did my research. I know all about you," says Conor in a smug tone, going up a step to get closer to me. I take a step back to maintain my distance. "How you uncovered the SHA fraternity, how you almost died doing it, how utterly amazed the nation was to see a 19-year-old freshman at a small university solve a decades-old mystery." I raise an eyebrow as Conor looks into my eyes. "I agree with them. It's unbelievable."

"Do you do this to everyone you meet?" I say jokingly, breaking eye contact with him and opening the door to the top floor. Conor laughs and leads the way.

"Just did my homework, that's all." Conor pops his head into an empty room. Simply looking inside of it gives me chills. I try to suppress the memory of tearing through boxes of plaques last year, digging for some shred of evidence surrounding the case with my roommate, Drew, and the old Student Manager, Ryker. After the entire thing went to court, the higher-ups at WRDW decided to box up all the Greek life plaques that lived in this room and leave them on the curb. Now, the room is only home to dust bunnies and a spiderweb in a corner. "What was in here?"

"Nothing. They're thinking of installing more computers so we can edit up here," I say, making something up on the spot. I walk past the room and hear Conor's footsteps follow me down the hallway. "Peter moved his office up here. If you're ever in trouble, you'll go into that room," I say, gesturing to the door with Peter's name on it.

"Let's hope that never happens," says Conor. "How about you? Have you ever been sent up here?"

"To his office? Yeah," I say.

"For the SHA investigation?" I stop walking and turn around, not enjoying his shameless prying. Conor puts his hands in his pockets and looks at me with a little smug smile on his face as though he knows exactly what he's doing.

"If you know everything about me, you'll know the answer to that question," I say. "I'm showing you around right now. This is your time to ask me questions about the station, not about me." Conor smiles down at me. "What?"

"You always this kind to new interns?" he asks. My knee-jerk reaction to his snarky remark is to dismiss him on the spot, but I manage to muster up some more patience.

"Let's keep going," I decide as Conor snickers. I take him down the stairs on the other side of the hallway and back into the main lobby of the building. Walking him past the front door, I approach a wall of clear windows and one clear door, behind which are three more doors to separate rooms. "The three doors there are the studios. If you're ever asked to read something on air, that's where you'll do it. Considering you'll be doing writing for your first year, I don't think you'll ever need to go in there."

"So, will you be giving me stories to write about?" Conor asks.

"Yep. I'll give you an interview someone else recorded, and you'll log it, write the story, pull soundbites, everything." Once we're back in the lobby, I put my hands on my hips and try to remember if I've left out anything. "I think that's about it for the building. Let me get your phone number in case I need to call you for anything." I take out my phone and hand it to him.

"Only business?" Conor asks with a mischievous smile.

"*Strictly* business," I say, once again suppressing the urge to kick him out of the front door. "You've sufficiently stalked me. You must know I have a boyfriend." Conor finishes typing in his number and hands my phone back to me.

"I do. I also know boyfriends come and go." I try not to glare at him as he smirks.

"Like interns," I say calmly back. The smirk on his face falls somewhat but stubbornly persists. Not breaking eye contact, I give him his station card. "This will get you into the building on your next shift. Text me if it doesn't work." Conor takes it from me and slips it into his pocket. "Any last questions?"

"I think I'm good," says Conor. He bites his lip lightly. It probably makes girls swoon, but it just makes my hand itch to slap him. "Thanks for the tour, Brooklyn. See you later." He hikes up the collar of his black coat, stuffs his hands in his pockets, winks, and leaves out of the front door, glancing back over his shoulder to confirm I'm still standing there watching him go.

^^^

After I open the door to my apartment, I toss my keys on the flimsy kitchen table made of manufactured wood, and the door swings shut behind me, locking me inside. I'm greeted by silence, so I decide to break it.

"Hello? Anyone home?" I call. Looking for something to munch on, I go into the kitchen that's full of cheap laminate surfaces. Drew pops out of her room, the black hair of her side bang covering her left eye. She's snacking on pretzels, holding a giant family-sized bag.

"Heya. How was the station?" she asks, opening the fridge and grabbing her water bottle.

"Good. I met my intern."

"Is he cute?"

"*He* thinks he is," I say. "I think he was trying to hit on me, actually." Drew laughs and takes a swig of water. "Took everything I had not to smack him and tell him to leave."

"You're a minor celebrity, Brook. He probably thinks you're hot."

"Who thinks Brook is hot?" Kennedy has arrived. She grabs an apple from the bowl of mostly overripe fruit on the counter. "I mean, they'd be correct." I manage to squeeze my way out of our small kitchen and lean in the open doorway to the living room.

"Thanks, Kenni. It's my new intern at WRDW," I fill in.

"What's his year?" Kenni asks.

"He's a freshman."

"Does he know about Nate?" Drew says.

"Probably."

"Ugh, way to make a good first impression. He should be nothing but respectful to you," says Kenni.

"Someone's got to tell him that." I muse over the thought. "And if he doesn't shape up, that someone will be me."

"Hell yeah, it will," Drew approves, eating another pretzel. The apartment becomes quiet. It has been a while since we've all been home together. Usually, Kenni is in the library studying, I'm at the radio station, and Drew is in the art studio. It feels nice to be home like a family again. There's a knock on the door that my roommates don't seem to hear over Kenni's crunchy bite into an apple.

"I'll get it!" I say, walking over to our front door. When I open it, I see Finn standing on the other side. He has his black hood over his head and shivers where he stands.

"You were gonna leave me out there to freeze!" he accuses me jokingly as he comes inside and takes off his shoes. When he shakes the hood off his head, his blonde hair catches the light.

"Oh yeah, in the ten-second walk you have from across the balcony there, you were going to die," I mock, shutting the door behind him. Drew puts down her bag of pretzels and comes to hug her boyfriend.

"Hey, hey," she happily chirps, kissing him on the cheek.

"No, don't kiss me! I'm like a metal pole. You'll freeze to me," Finn says with a smile, kissing her on the head. "What are you guys up to?"

"Brook was telling us about her new intern at the station," Kenni relays. Finn sits at the table, his black wet coat soaking the chair beneath him. He puts his socked feet on the table but puts them back down on the ground when I give him a pointed look.

"Yeah? He as charming as me?" asks Finn.

"So he thinks," I mutter.

"What's his name?" Drew asks.

"Conor Valree."

"Just an innocent freshman?" Finn says.

"An innocent freshman who seems to know all about me," I say, going back into the kitchen and grabbing a bag of dried mango slices.

"What do you mean?" Finn calls. I return to the living room and sit on the frayed blue couch next to Kenni.

"He basically relayed my freshman year to me. Seems like he's done his research," I tell them.

"I'm not a journalism kid. Is that a normal thing for you guys to do?" Finn asks.

"Is it *normal* to read me my entire life story? No, not at all," I say.

"That's kinda creepy," Kenni remarks. I nod and eat a slice of mango.

"You think?" I say sarcastically.

"Let's hope he doesn't end up like Taylor," Drew says in a lighter tone. It's meant to be a joke, but the room goes quiet as the image of Taylor's twisted grin pops into our minds.

Last year, watching Taylor's sentencing at the end of the spring semester had rattled all of us. What was truly disturbing was the way he stayed stone-faced the entire time as if the trial and the verdict were all just parts of his plan. I remember his mother bursting into tears and his father hopelessly attempting to comfort her as their son stood behind the defendant's table in a puke-green jumpsuit.

"At least Taylor didn't let on how much he knew about me," I point out in the silence. "Conor's got an odd vibe. I can't really put my finger on it." Finn goes to search the cabinets for food. I hear the cabinets banging shut as he realizes his limited snack options.

"You guys don't have Pringles?" he calls.

"You ate them all!" says Drew.

"Buy your own damn Pringles!" says Kenni as I eat another mango slice with a laugh. There's another knock on the door. No one makes a move toward it.

"Really?" Drew dramatically huffs, making the effort to turn and yank open the knob. In the few seconds the door is open, a blast of cold air blows into our apartment.

"Snowin' like hell out there!" says my boyfriend, stamping his boots outside of the door before coming in. I swallow the piece of mango I'm chewing and go to give him a hug. Nate hugs me back eagerly and a breath of relief escapes him. "God, you're so warm."

"You're covered in snow! Take off your coat," I tell him, releasing him from my bear hug. Nate carelessly throws the black cargo jacket on the chair next to Finn.

"Hey dude," greets Nate, readjusting the bottom of his shirt and jerking his chin upwards at Finn as a greeting.

"Hey," Finn replies. Drew, Kenni, and I share a pointed look. Although the two of them aren't the best of friends yet, they're more tolerant of each other than they were last year. At the very least, we can get through a conversation without Nate accusing Finn of being subversive. Nate takes a seat next to me on the couch and puts his arm around me.

"The house is totally gone. Issac told me," Nate says.

"Oh, right. They tore the house down today," Kenni remembers. She bites her fingernail. "How is, uh, Issac, by the way?"

"Still good, Kenni." Nate smiles. Kenni nods and crosses one leg over the other, attempting to look uninterested.

"Good, that's good to hear," she waves away with the same air. Nate kisses me on the head.

"It's finally over," he comforts me, glancing out of the window with me at the snow weaving a thick blanket on the ground. I can only grimace and nod, not wanting to say anything aloud for the fear of being jinxed once again.

2

Something glints in the infinite darkness above my head.
"You stupid thing, Brooklyn Perce."
The knife is pressing into my skull.
"Should've gotten out when you had the chance."
His grey eyes glint as the knife comes down in a flash of light.

"AH!" I scream, bolting up in bed and steadying myself by placing my hands behind me. I look around my room wildly, in search of Taylor's twisted face. I find no one.

I lean against the wall and put my head back, shutting my eyes. When I roll over to check my phone, the screen tells me it's three a.m. I have an alarm set for eight. My brain needs the sleep, but I don't think I can even rest. I gather my blanket around me and stare at the wall, trying to focus on the photos I've covered it with.

The nightmares started just before the trial. I would dream about Taylor and the other boys. Sometimes, they piled on me, like animals, until I suffocated. At other times, they trapped me in an old closet in the house and waited for me to starve. On select nights, I dreamt about Ryker kissing me with poison on his lips, and as I faded away, Taylor would madly cackle. My subconscious has been trained to try to snap me out of a nightmare when I can recognize I'm in one, but otherwise, there's no escape from the horrors in my head.

And though I thought being back at school would end the issue, it decidedly didn't. If anything, being closer to where everything happened, having to pass the damn house every day, makes things worse. I would wake up from a nightmare in the middle of the night, and I would call on Nate. He always kept his phone on vibrate by his head so if I happened to text, he would wake up. He would run to the other side of our small apartment building and cuddle with me until morning. The next day before returning to his apartment, he would make sure I was okay. After a while, I promised myself not to text him at night because I could tell he was tired all the time. As much as he tried to hide it, there was no mistaking his yawning every twenty seconds.

But this dream ...

Never have I been killed so quickly in a dream. My death is typically drawn out because the boys want a good show. I would give them one, crying and screaming and pleading for them to let me go, the exact opposite of what I did when I was actually trapped in the house. When I wake up, I'm either sweating or on the verge of tears. Once I was sobbing in my sleep, and Kenni heard it from her room next door. She was horrified when she shook me awake that night.

I hunker back down in my bed and put my head on the pillow. When I was little, my mom used to tell me to count backwards from one hundred to put myself to sleep. "If you say it slowly and soothingly, you'll drift off, in no time," she said. So that's what I do.

100 ...

99 ...

98 ...

97 ...

^^^

Later in the day, I run to the business school to deliver the form that will officially declare my minor in marketing. While my parents love my being a broadcast journalism major, they want to see me minor in something "marketable," so marketing was a natural choice.

I've never been in Fraanco before, but it's just as modern as Rosenburg, with large glass windows, expansive study spaces, and kids with noses buried in their laptops, madly typing away on spreadsheets. The only difference is in people's attire. Here, everyone looks like they're about to go to the interviews of their lives. I suddenly feel underdressed in my boots, grey sweater, and jeans.

I make my way to the advising office and open the sleek wood door. Two students sit behind a desk next to a hallway that leads to the offices of the faculty advisors. The rest of the waiting area holds a few chairs, a case of paperwork on one wall, and a photo of the front of the building on another wall. One of the students behind the desk, a male, looks up when I approach the desk.

"Hi. How can I help you?" he greets.

"Hey, I was just wondering if someone could sign this minor declaration form for me. I'm from Rosenburg," I explain. Once I mention I'm from the communication school, the boy's smile drops a bit. Fraanco and Rosenburg are constantly locked in a duel for which can be the most prestigious school. I'm technically behind enemy lines, just standing here.

"You'd have to meet with Professor Carthwrite, and he's in with a student right now. Have a seat," he says, giving me a side eye as I sit down. "I'll let him know someone's here to see him." I put my backpack on the ground and lean back, looking around the tidy reception room.

"You're from Rosenburg?" asks a new voice. I turn my head to my right and see the other occupant of the waiting area, a boy with light chestnut-colored hair. I can tell his standing height is on the taller side by the way his legs sort of crumple on the floor. What weirds me out are his eyes: grey with black flecks in his irises. They would be ghostly if he wasn't sort of smiling. The way he twists his lips in a contorted grin makes my stomach hurt. Only one other person I used to know smiled like that.

"Yeah, I'm a journalism major," I tell the boy while trying to stop my heart from beating rapidly. Something in my gut doesn't like this boy, despite the friendly smile on his face. He reminds me too much of Taylor. That alone is enough to make me tense.

"I'm minoring in Rosenburg. Advertising," he clarifies. He offers his hand out to me. "Gavin Wryte." I stare at his outstretched palm. He doesn't seem dangerous, but I can't let myself be too careful. Once he raises an eyebrow, I realize I'm being rude.

"Brooklyn Perce." I take his hand tentatively and shake it once. Gavin looks like he's wondering where he knows my name from, and I stifle an exasperated groan. I know what he's going to say.

"That name's familiar. You, uh, you busted the frat, right?"

"Guilty," I grit through my teeth, attempting to hide my annoyance. *Why did I say my last name? Just 'Brooklyn' would've been fine.*

"Must've taken nerve," he says almost enviously. I just nod. There's silence between us. I hate talking about the past. I already relive it enough in my subconscious. I don't need to reminisce every time I meet someone new. Gavin's head is still turned to me, studying the side of my face. *Why's he looking at me like that?* My heart beats faster, and my brain screams at me to leave. I look at him with a confused expression, pushing down the urge to sprint away.

"Can I help you with something?" I question, my words coming out ruder than I mean them to. Gavin shakes his head, his eyes still fixed on me.

"No. Just ... It's nothing," he says nonchalantly, turning his body forwards and staring at the opposite wall. Something about his slow deliberate movement spooks me. The uncomfortable feeling I've been getting in waves suddenly overwhelms me, suffocating every fiber in my body. I gather my things, stand abruptly, and put my minor declaration form on the main desk.

"Give this to the professor, please," I tell the receptionist urgently. The boy opens his mouth to retort, but I'm too fast. I turn on my booted heels and walk briskly out of the office, feeling Gavin's eyes burn holes into the small of my back. As soon as I leave the room, I can breathe freely again.

I burst out of the front doors of the college and instinctively hug myself, shielding my chest against the cold air. I didn't bring a heavy jacket, even though

I should know better by now. I slip on my light leather jacket and zip it up, biting my lips as I walk towards the counseling center.

Northwich is usually cold in the fall, but ever since November hit, it feels more like January. I wish it were already January, so I could get on a bus and go home to celebrate my birthday with my mom and my dog, Harley. Mom says my grandparents may come this year. I could definitely use a hug from my grandpa who always squeezes me too tightly and a kiss on the forehead from my grandma who always remarks on how tall I've gotten since their last visit. We could sit around and play games while Harley would nudge my hand, begging for pets. As I think of the "death by chocolate cake" my mom always makes on my birthday, I feel my mouth water. A blast of frigid air to my face reminds me I'm here instead, where name recognition and an uncharacteristic nervousness follow me everywhere.

Ring ring. Ring ring.

My hand dives into my pocket and brings out my phone. When I see who's calling, I feel my heart sink. It's my dad. I haven't picked up one of his calls in a while. In fact, I've been purposefully avoiding him for the sake of my mental health. As much as she doesn't like him, my mom would tell me I have to pick up once in a while just to let him know I'm at the very least alive. Reluctantly, I press 'Pick up.'

"Hello?" I say, my teeth chattering.

"Hello, honey. How are you?" asks my dad politely. From the background noise I hear, he must be driving home.

"Fine. Freezing. How are you?"

"I'm doing well. How's the radio station? Still working hard?" *Well that didn't take long.* I let out a measured breath through my nose.

"Yeah, Dad, I'm working. Don't worry."

"Good. Working's important. Hey, listen. I called to talk to you about something."

I stop walking and wait for the stoplight to turn red, so I can cross the street. I pace in place to stay warm. The other students gathering around me seem to have the same idea.

"What's that?"

"The firm I work for is having a summit this weekend, up in Northwich. I'm coming up tomorrow and staying until Sunday. Do you have any plans?" he asks, a tint of hope in his voice. I heave a sigh and see my breath hit the cold air. My feet keep marching in place.

"No," I answer truthfully after a pause.

"I was thinking we could do something. Go to dinner, see a movie, whatever you want to do. I know the mall is nice up there. We could do some shopping if you'd like." I can't believe what I'm hearing. My dad makes money to hoard it. Is he really offering to spend money on me beyond his legal obligations? I nod, but I don't know to whom.

"Yeah, that would be great. You could meet my friends," I offer.

"I would love that." It sounds forced. "Does tomorrow work for you?"

"No, I'm hanging with Kenni and Drew tomorrow night. Saturday maybe?"

"Sounds like a plan. I'll text you when I arrive tomorrow."

"Okay, Dad," I say, seeing the counseling center on my left.

"Can't wait to see you, honey. Love you," he says, though I can hear the tinge of fake excitement in his tone.

"Love you too, Dad." I only half mean it. I hang up and open the huge wooden door, hearing the familiar creaking of the hinges and the wood.

Like the Campus Police office, the counseling center used to be someone's house before the university bought it out from under the owner. The entire place has a calm aura, with a scent of lavender and chamomile and ambient nature sounds playing softly over the speakers that are lodged in the old mahogany ceiling. I walk up to the slender woman behind the front desk and wait for her to finish typing before I say anything. She looks up at me with a pleasant soft smile.

"Brooklyn Perce here to see Margaret," I say. The woman quickly types something in on her computer.

"Alright, have a seat, Ms. Perce. Margaret will be with you shortly," whispers the woman, leaning in like it's a secret. I nod in thanks and go back towards the waiting area. I'm about to flop down in one of the cushy chairs when I hear Margaret's voice.

"Brooklyn! I'm ready for you." I hike up my bag over my shoulder and follow her down the hallway to the right of the front desk. We enter her office, and she shuts the door behind me.

Much like her, Margaret's office is very orderly. Not a book on her shelf is askew, the surface of her desk is clear except for a laptop, and all the mountain pictures, hung on the walls, are equally spaced. It's not a large office, but the window beside her desk makes the room look marginally bigger. Through the old glass pane, I can see students gleefully walking by. I wish I were one of them.

"How are you, Brooklyn?" asks Margaret, in a motherly tone, as I make myself comfortable in the padded chair adjacent to her desk.

"I'm doing well. How are you?" I respond politely.

"Alright. It's been one of *those* days, you know," she says in her quiet tone. She crosses one booted leg over another and tugs down her skirt to make sure it's in place. "How's everything been going?"

I shrug half-heartedly and avoid looking at her. Instead, my eyes search the wall behind her and then drift to admire the leaves that are still clinging to the trees outside of her window.

"Pretty good. I'm doing fine. I honestly don't know why I come here," I say half-jokingly. Margaret nods and smiles with her wine-colored lips.

"Lots of kids say that on good days. It's the bad ones when they need me," she says. I nod. Margaret looks at the legal pad on her lap with handwritten notes that only doctors could read. "You said last time you were experiencing intense nightmares. Is that still the case?" The memory of my night terror flashes before my eyes so vividly and so fiercely that it almost hurts. Nevertheless, I shake my head.

"No. In fact, I haven't had one in a while," I lie.

"Really?" Margaret narrows her eyes as I remain fixed on life outside the office window.

"Yeah."

"Brooklyn, I know when you're lying." Now, I look her in the eyes. She appears discouraged that I would even think about lying to her. "You've been coming to me for the past year, and you're still lying to me."

"I thought you weren't supposed to judge, only listen," I say, trying not to sound annoyed. Margaret raises an eyebrow. I have clearly failed to temper my tone. "Sorry." I look out of the window again. One of the leaves I was eyeing has fallen.

"It's alright. If you don't want to talk about it, then we don't have to," Margaret tells me, recomposing herself. I know she's saying that to make me feel better, but I can't help it when memories of last night's dream invade my consciousness.

"I still see things in my dreams ...Well, not dreams. They're more like nightmares. He ... He finds me wherever I am. I could be in a field of sunflowers, and he'll come find me and take me away. Usually, he drags out my death, and it lasts the entire night until my alarm clock rings. But ... last night was different."

"How so?"

"He took a knife and just killed me." I shake my head slightly, smiling at how stupid it sounds and how I'm tearing up just hearing the words. "And, in a way, I was kind of thankful for it being so fast. I was happy that he went for it and didn't hold back."

Margaret appears to be so horrified that she doesn't write anything down. I continue. "That night in the house ... Sometimes, I replay the scene over and over, line by line until he grabs me by the throat, pins me to the wall, and squeezes. Except I don't live ... I die then too." I pause to let Margaret say something, but she only nods, encouraging me to go on. "I guess part of me thinks I should've died. Part of me thinks I'm lucky. And the other part thinks there's a reason why I lived."

"If you had to pick which one of these parts was the most dominant, could you?" Margaret prods. There's silence as I think about my answer.

"No," I croak out. My throat is dry from thinking aloud and breathing out of my mouth. I swallow for the first time in what feels like hours. Margaret gives me a small smile.

"I'm happy you're still with us. You deserve a better life than the one you had last year, a better college experience as well." I nod in agreement.

"I know, but I'm still jumpy. I'm still so untrusting of strangers. Whenever I meet someone new, there's the little thought in the back of my head, like 'What if they're trying to kill you?' I never used to be like this." My face betrays my disgust at myself. "I hate being like this. I want it to stop." It sounds childish when I say it, but I don't know how else to put it.

"You've experienced a traumatic event, Brooklyn. It's not going to get better overnight. There's going to be an adjustment period here. You have to let yourself heal," Margaret advises gently. I say nothing. Instead, I study my cuticles which have seen better days. Margaret looks down and checks her notes as I look outside again. There are fewer people socializing and the wind has blown more leaves down from the tree.

"Everything in your waking life is as usual?" Margaret wants to know.

I look back at her hopeful face again. All this woman wants is for me to be alright. That's why I lie. Even though she sees through it sometimes, I must present her with a comforting illusion. She helps ten to twenty students a day, most of whom are suffering from anxiety, homesickness, or depression. I like to think I'm the least of her problems, but, in reality, I'm probably near the top of her list. I nod in response.

"Yeah. My grades are fine, my roommates are great, and my boyfriend is doing well. My dad is visiting this weekend, so that should be fun."

"You'll tell me how it goes?"

I give Margaret a smile. "Do I have a choice?"

3

Instead of going home after my session, I go to Nate's apartment. West Campus has at least a hundred individual buildings that look like shipping crates. Depending on the building, each one has eight double or triple apartments. My friends and I chose to live in the same crate, so it's easy to visit one another. I live in the end apartment on the top right. Nate lives in the apartment on the top left.

My feet take me up the stairs, and my hand turns the knob to let me into his apartment. For an apartment full of guys, it's very clean. Some of the walls are covered by posters depicting various movies, sports players, and animals. A street sign that says 'NO PARKING ANYTIME' hangs above the TV. Nate still refuses to tell me where he got the sign from. A massive Delta Rho fraternity flag, surrounded by pictures of Nate, his roommates, his other brothers, and his friends at various events, adorns the largest wall. I'm proud to report I've made the wall at least four times.

Nate's head pops out of the hallway, and his smile grows when he sees me. He's not wearing a shirt, which is appropriate because the apartment is just shy of 85 degrees, but it feels like heaven to me.

"Hey!" he says happily, coming over and hugging me.

"H-hey," I shiver, hugging myself again in an effort to keep warm.

"You look like you're going to freeze over," Nate laughs, taking my backpack from me and placing it on the floor.

"G-g-great observation," I say with a tight smile, my lips unable to move. Nate smirks and kisses my cheek.

"If there's one thing I'm good at, it's making observations," he jokes. He kisses me again, this time on the lips, then lets me go, and walks to the kitchen to put milk in a cup.

"W-what are you d-doing?" I chatter, walking with him.

"Making you hot cocoa because I'm a good boyfriend." Nate empties the cup of milk into a pot and turns on the stove.

"He's *the best* boyfriend," says Issac, walking into the kitchen and taking a box of Cheerios from the cabinet.

Issac's auburn hair is currently in a mop on the top of his head, and his green eyes are framed by thick plastic glasses. He's wearing a sweatshirt with sweatpants that, by the looks of them, haven't been washed in a while. Adding to his frazzled appearance are the holes in his right sock. One little peek into his room, and I can see textbooks, papers, binders, and an open laptop on his desk.

"Damn straight," says Nate, making a kissing sound with his lips in Issac's direction. Issac returns the gesture and leans on the wall opposite where I'm leaning.

"Drowning in homework?" I ask him.

"All day, every day. It's like they *want* me to give up." He throws a handful of Cheerios into his mouth and munches. Issac is a mechanical engineering major, so he rarely ever comes out of his room, unless there's a Delta Rho event, in which case, Issac is first in line at the keg. "Where'd you come from?"

"Fraanco. I tried to declare my minor."

"How did that go?"

"Fine, until some freshman kept ogling me, and I got the hell out of there," I say.

"Well, that's fun," Issac says. He looks at Nate. "You worried about this?"

"If it's one thing Brook has showed me, it's that she can take care of herself," says Nate.

"He's a freshman. What's the worst he can do?" I ask Issac.

"Make you live in a dorm again," he muses. I giggle at him as Cheerios fall out of his mouth. Whenever I come to this apartment, I always find myself laughing.

"How much chocolate do you want in it?" Nate asks, pouring the milk back into the mug and placing the pot in the sink.

"A lot," I say. Nate considers my request for a moment, then dumps what I estimate to be a third of a cup of Nesquik into the mug. He starts stirring, and a poof of chocolate powder escapes the white rim.

"Smooth," Issac jokes.

"She said a lot!" Nate defends.

"She didn't say the whole damn carton, Stevenson!" Issac says. He shakes his head like he's ashamed of his roommate. "Your boyfriend has the brawn, but not the brains."

"I still love him," I say, taking the cup from his hands and kissing him on the cheek.

"And I'm still alone," Issac jokingly gripes.

"Dude, I'm telling you. Her roommate, Kennedy, is into you," Nate informs him. Issac squints and shakes his head.

"She must have the wrong Issac. Girls don't like me. I remind them too much of their exes." Issac thinks for a second. "Well, that or I just work all the time, so I can't really take people out."

"I can give you her number if you want. She'd be happy to hear from you," I offer, sipping the hot cocoa. The chocolaty goodness runs down my throat and coats my mouth. Issac looks like he's considering it and then shakes his head again like he's being foolish.

"Maybe some other time. I have a lot of work," he says. Issac puts the Cheerios back in the cabinet and brushes his hands off on his pants. "Have fun, kids."

"Bye, Issac!" I call as he retreats into his study cave. When the door shuts, Nate walks into his room at the opposite end of the hallway, and I follow.

My boyfriend's room is the same layout as mine, but smaller. I was lucky to get the biggest bedroom in my apartment, but he wasn't. His desk and dresser are crammed onto one wall, so when the door swings inward, it hits the chest of drawers. The deep blue comforter on his bed is in a heap at one end of the mattress, and his pillows are scattered around the top. His laptop is open to Netflix where a TV episode is paused. His shut closet doors hide hundreds of shirts and jackets he has stashed away. There are two pairs of shoes scattered on the floor, but other than that, his room is neat. I sip my cocoa and sit on his bed. Nate sits on his desk chair, his legs straddling the back. He leans forward and looks at me, narrowing his eyes.

"Something's wrong," he says. I don't say anything. "What's wrong, Brook?"

"My dad called, Nate," I huff with tight lips, staring down at my lap and watching the steam curl into the air from the mug. Nate's eyes slightly widen.

"Why?"

"He's coming into town tomorrow. Something about work. He says he's staying the entire weekend and wants me to hang out with him on Saturday."

"You're going to?"

"I mean, yeah." I take another sip. "He's my dad. I haven't seen him since school started."

"Am I gonna get to meet him?"

"Only if you want to. I didn't mention I had a boyfriend," I say. Nate raises his eyebrows.

"Do *you* want me to?" Nate asks after a second. I don't answer immediately, and Nate throws up a hand in exasperation. "Well you just answered my question."

"I just ... I don't want him to think I'm wasting my time," I say.

"Why would he think that? I'm sure I'll be fine —"

"You don't know him," I tell Nate, finally looking up from my lap. I clutch the mug harder. "He'd tear you to shreds if he knew you existed."

"Brook, he should be proud of you. What did he say when he heard about the frat?"

"He wasn't thrilled I put my life in danger, let me say that much," I concede after a beat. "Besides, the frat thing didn't make me any money which is always his main concern."

"You didn't get money for interviews?" Nate asks.

"No one's paying a 19-year-old for anything unless you apply for it. Even then, it's a long shot."

"True." There's a pause. "So, what are you going to do with him?"

"Go out to dinner, I guess. It's gonna be awful."

"Hey, you get free food. Look at it that way." When I'm not amused by his joke, Nate gets up and comes over to me. He kneels on the ground and looks up at me. In the light coming in from his window, his eyes look like browned honey, deep and amber. Nate smiles reassuringly. "I'll be there for you, alright? If you feel uncomfortable, just call. I'll come pick you up. I'll take Issac's car. He won't mind. Alright?" I nod and give him a little smile.

"You're the best," I praise. Nate kisses me lightly.

"Yeah, I know," he mutters. We both break out into bigger smiles, and Nate takes the mug I'm holding to put it on the floor. He takes me by the hands and just stares at me with all the care in the world. My heart, normally fluttering due to nerves and worry, finally slows to a healthy pace. "Love you, Brooklyn."

"Love you, Nate." I kiss him again and again until my lips hurt, not wanting to go back home.

4

I open the door to my apartment and slowly close it behind me, trying to bring order to my messy hair before my roommates notice I'm home. In the living room, I tip-toe around, attempting to be quiet as I get my life together. Unfortunately, Kennedy comes around the corner and raises an eyebrow when she sees the state I'm in.

"Hey," I say cheerfully, giving her a huge grin.

"Heyyyy," she drags out, trying to suppress laughter.

"Did Brook just get some?" Drew calls from her room. I roll my eyes, but the huge grin on my face stays.

"I think so, Drew!" Kenni calls back, watching as I go down the hallway in a huff. "Care to comment, Brook?"

"What do we have to eat?" I ask loudly. I push past Kenni in the hall and look through the cabinets, ignoring my roommates.

"Let's see. What's on the menu?" Kenni says, propping herself in the doorway of the kitchen as I ponder making pasta. "We have ramen, hamburgers, and a tall glass of water which you need after what you just did."

"Alright, you can stop," I say as Kenni and Drew laugh.

"I'm proud of you," yells Drew from her room.

"Yeah, I mean I'm going on three months without anything, and I'm forgetting everything," says Kenni.

"Until you hook up with Issac. Then you'll be on track," Drew teases.

"Oh, I mentioned you to Issac today!" I say, happy to change the subject. Kenni's face lights up.

"How is he!"

"I offered to give him your number, but he said he had a lot of work to do and went back to his room," I explain, taking a microwaveable mac and cheese from the cabinet and filling it with water.

"Yeah, he's got a lot of work to do ... *on me*!" Kenni says, like it's obvious.

"He's an engineer. Give him a break," I remind her.

"I'm a poly sci major. I have plenty of time when I'm not in the library ... which is never," she says. I give her a pointed look.

"Sorry, Kenni, looks like you're on your own on this one," I say.

"Hasn't deterred me yet," says Kenni proudly. The microwave beeps, and I add the packet of 'cheese' to the pasta and stir. The smell is nauseating, and the pasta inside the plastic cup tastes like cardboard, but I really don't feel like washing dishes. I start walking to my room, then stop myself, turning back around.

"Oh, hey, my dad is coming on Saturday," I say casually. "Thought you guys should know." That causes Drew to get out of her chair and stand in the doorway, a shocked expression plastered on her make-up laden face. Kenni also turns around with both of her eyebrows raised. I take a bite of my cardboard dinner and look at them innocently. They're more disturbed about my father's random pop-in than I am.

"When did *this* happen?" Drew asks incredulously.

"A few hours ago. He called and said he had business stuff in Northwich, and he's gonna be here for a couple days. He wants to come to campus and take me out to dinner."

"And you're just gonna *let* him come here?" Kenni says, perplexed.

"It's not like I'm border control for Northwich. He's got the right to go wherever he wants."

"Brook, the only thing you do is talk shit about your father who, if I remember correctly, broke up with your mom because he was hoarding money from her," Drew says to me.

"You don't have to remind me, dude. I'm just going out to dinner with him. That's all. In a way, I'm taking back the money I'm owed." When I enter my room, I shouldn't have shut the door behind me because Kenni comes in right after I do.

"Hey. You wanna talk about it?" Kenni asks gently like the sweetheart she is. "'Cause you don't have to do anything you don't want to, alright?"

"I know." Kenni is quiet. "You want to know the first thing he asked me when I picked up the phone, other than how I was?"

"What?"

"If I still had my job." I try to suppress an annoyed look on my face. "He's my dad, and I know I should love him. I just … I hate how he's obsessed with money."

"I would hate it too," sympathizes Kenni.

"He just …" I sigh and run a hand through my hair. "He's always hid everything from me and my mom. I hate it. If he stopped, I would forgive him. He just hasn't. That's the only way he knows how to make people like him … bragging about his job and his money." Kenni just stands in the doorway of my room, her hands shoved in her pockets. "I spend every holiday with my mom because he'll try to tell me the price of everything that he's bought me, which is usually two small gifts that together cost about fifty bucks … I figure just let him buy me dinner tomorrow, and that'll be the end of it."

"I'm sorry, Brook," says Kenni, in a small voice.

"Don't be. Not your fault he's a materialistic asshole." I take the last bite of mac and cheese and then throw out the plastic cup in my trash can. My hand rips my towel off the back of my door. "I'm going to take a shower. Then I'm going to sleep."

^^^

Knock, knock.

"Brooklyn?" asks Penelope, a meek little freshman, who oddly reminds me of a sparrow. I look up from the story I'm reading to see her standing in the threshold of the newsroom. "There's someone here for you."

"Who?" I say.

"He said he's your intern."

"Alright." I hug myself as I get a sudden chill. I'm still wearing the same sweatshirt I was wearing yesterday. It's Nate's. I stole it since I threw my shirt on the floor after yesterday's visit. It has the yellow Delta Rho Greek letters stitched onto the royal blue fabric. Its fleece lining smells like his cologne and makes me feel safe, like I'm wrapped in Nate's constant and reassuring embrace. Penelope nods and walks away. She's replaced by Conor with the usual sneaky grin on his face.

"Hey, Brooklyn," he says casually.

"Hey. Not that I don't like you stopping by, but it's Friday evening. Shouldn't you be pre-gaming by now?" I say. Conor smiles and leans against my desk.

"You would think, but no. I was just walking by and wanted to see if you were in."

"Well, I'm here. What's up?" His upper lip twitches.

"Can't I just say hello?"

"Let's be honest with each other, Conor. What is it?"

"Am I allowed to write stories that you don't give me?" he asks. I finally turn to him and look him in his green eyes. Something about staring into them for too long makes me uncomfortable. It reminds me how I felt staring into Gavin's eyes yesterday.

"Depends. What story do you have in mind?"

"If I ever find anything interesting that someone here isn't already covering."

"If it's relevant to the community, sure." I narrow my eyes. "That can't be the only reason why you came here." Conor shrugs and bites his bottom lip like he's guilty. I search his face, becoming even more uncomfortable with the look in his eyes. *Get him out of here. Say whatever you must. Just make him leave.*

"You're a good journalist. Not better than me, though," Conor says. He crosses his arms and looks down at me. "There's something wrong with you. I can see it in your beautiful eyes."

"Alright," I snap, standing to get away from him. Conor raises an eyebrow, and the smirk on his face grows. "You can't be saying that sort of stuff to me. I'm your mentor. And I have a boyfriend." I gesture to the sweatshirt that's clearly too long on me.

"Kinda figured a pretty girl like you would be taken. They all are."

"What do you want, Conor?" Conor doesn't seem deterred by my indignant tone.

"Your boyfriend, he's in DR?"

"Yeah."

"A friend of mine wants to rush."

"You want me to give your friend Nate's number?"

"So that's his name." I scoff at him.

"You seriously think that's an okay question to ask?"

"Well, yeah." There's silence again.

"No," I finally say.

"Why not?"

"Rushing politics isn't something I want to be involved in." Conor smirks.

"Think of it as a favor."

"I don't want you to owe me anything." At my remark, my trainee purses his lips.

"I see."

BZZZZ. BZZZZ. BZZZZ.

My phone vibrates on the table next to Conor. He glances down at it and sees the caller ID which reads 'Dad'. Conor's eyes flick back up to me.

"Is this why you're so jumpy?" I don't say anything. "Dad's coming to town?"

"Yes, actually, he is."

"When's he coming?"

"Tomorrow night."

"Where are you two going?"

"Leave, Conor," I bark in a loud voice as he finally gets on my last nerve. He still has that same infuriating, lazy half-smile.

"As you wish." Conor walks backwards out of the newsroom, maintaining eye contact the entire time. Even as I try to remain calm, the urge to slap him remains. An infuriating half-smile gleams on his face as he leaves. "See you Monday, Brooklyn Perce."

BZZZZZ. BZZZZZ. BZZZZ.

I still don't pick up the phone.

5

The night before dinner with my father, Kenni, Drew, Finn, and I are sitting around our living room with drinks in our hands. I'm sipping a Vodka Lemonade, and I'm at the point when I can no longer taste the drink. Luckily, I've never been an outgoing drunk. I usually sit quietly and think about life for a while, maybe while listening to music if I feel up to it. Kenni, meanwhile, is playing Mario Kart on our Nintendo Switch as the cuddling Finn and Drew watch. I'm just sitting on the floor, watching Yoshi's cart speed around the track on screen. I feel like I'm entranced, but something in me doesn't allow me to relax for long. I suddenly stand up and put down my drink.

"You good?" asks Drew lazily.

"I'm going to sleep. I'm tired," I declare. Drew sweeps her hand toward the hallway.

"Then, by all means. We'll see you tomorrow."

I make my way down the hall, my feet catching up to the rest of my body, so I half stumble across the floor. Whenever I'm like this, my bed looks irresistible. Part of me is compelled to call Nate or even go visit him, but I don't want to be any more of a burden to him than I already am. I need to let him have his own life.

Once I change out of my clothes and into my pajamas, I collapse onto the mattress, the ceiling above me spinning slightly. I momentarily become hypnotized by the swirling stucco over my head. My legs slide under the covers, and my body curls up into a little ball, so I'm facing the corner my bed makes with the tapestry-covered wall. The pillows feel endlessly fluffy underneath my head, and I pass out almost immediately. One of the last thoughts I have before my brain shuts down is the vain hope that I won't have a nightmare. Not now, not in the state I'm in.

But, of course, I'm not lucky.

"Brooklyn!"

A flash of Nate's face.

"Brooklyn, run!"

A flash of him turning and running for the stairs.

I turn and see Ryker passed out on the floor behind me. His face is beaten to a pulp, almost to the point where it's unrecognizable. But I'd know him anywhere.

"Brooklyn, c'mon!"

I turn back to see Nate looking at me wildly. He seems scared for his life, his chest rising and falling noticeably fast. Against my better judgement, I run to Ryker and drop to my knees, looking down at him. I don't know how I plan to help him. I just know I need to. All of a sudden, Ryker's face melts away like wax and shows Taylor's crude one underneath it. His eyes fly open, and I can see the whites of his eyes have turned crimson.

"GOTCHA!" I try to defend myself, but it's no use. Taylor's hands jump toward my throat, strangling me until I fall into nothing.

^^^

"Good morning. Well, I guess afternoon, now," greets Drew once I wake up the next day and shuffle out to the living room. She's sitting at the table, scrolling through something on her laptop, across from a girl whom I don't recognize. The girl is wearing the same green beanie and grey hoodie that Drew is wearing. Her makeup isn't as heavy as Drew's, and the way she sits indicates she's secure in herself. She turns to me and waves.

"Hi," she says in a slightly high-pitched voice.

"Hey," I greet back. After a look of confusion from me, Drew hops in.

"Brooklyn, this is Nicole from my pottery class. We suffer through it together," Drew explains.

"Tell me about it. Our professor is *such* a perfectionist," agrees Nicole.

"True, he's an ass."

"Remember when he said your vase was asymmetrical?" Nicole says, giggling at the memory.

"It was the *fifth* time I remade it! Art isn't meant to be perfect. He had it coming." At my questioning glance, Drew relents with a huff. "I smashed it on the floor in front of him and asked him to remake it the way he would like it. Bit of an overreaction, but I think I got my point across." I nod and pass the kitchen table as the two of them start laughing. Drew taps me on the arm as I go by, so I turn around. "Hey, you want some pasta? I made too much for lunch," Drew offers.

"I'll have some after I shower," I tell her. "It was nice meeting you, Nicole!"

"Likewise!" she says in a chipper voice.

When I open the door to my room, I half expect to see Nate on my bed. Usually, when he knows I've been having a bad day, he waits for me in my room and listens to me rant about whatever's on my mind until I get it all out. Then, he hugs me and offers to help me however he can. I don't know what I did to deserve him or what I keep doing for him that makes him stick around. The only thing I can offer in return is my judgment of others, and nowadays it seems I'm wrong more often than I'm right.

The hot water in the shower feels amazing running down my skin. Whenever I take a shower after I've had too much to drink, it feels like I'm being reborn. It's so refreshing, so calming, so clearing. I let the water hit my face and stand there for what feels like an eternity. My head is empty. I think about nothing besides my breathing. Until-

Taylor's eyes-

My neck twists to the side as his face flashes across my mind.

His cruel unforgiving laugh-

"No. No, no, no," I whisper to myself, putting my hands against the wall of the shower. The water hits the back of my neck as I squeeze my eyes shut.

His palms wrapped around my neck-

"No." I twitch my head to the left as though I can get the invisible hands off my throat. My hands run down my face, wiping off the water before the drops hit my skin again. "No, this isn't real." I shut off the shower and stand there a moment, dripping in the tub. My hand is still bracing my body against the wall as I stare down at my feet. With every breath out of my mouth, a little spray of water comes along with it. It's quiet as I listen to my heart pound, and it's this sound that makes me calm down slightly. When I can stand up on my own, I dry off and go back to my room.

I pull on a pair of dark wash jeans and a nice blouse to ready myself for dinner with my father. When I look in the mirror, I see my zitty face and all the scars I have from popping them. Stress zits run in the family, and there's been no shortage of stress lately. I'm tempted to pop a particularly red one that's partially hidden by my jaw, but I bite my short fingernails instead, which reminds me I need to file my nails. Dad would take one look at my raggedy hands and ask me why I haven't been taking care of myself. He notices the strangest things, my father. Always the little stuff, never the stuff that matters.

I give myself a once-over in the full-length mirror on the back of my closet door before sitting at my desk to apply makeup. I blend the hell out of my face to hide my blemishes from my dad. He would hate to see I'm breaking out. It's insane how he wants me to work hard and expects my appearance to stay the same. Half the time, I look like a mess, and I'm asleep the other half.

When I walk out of my room half an hour later, Drew is still at the table with Nicole, banging out homework. My roommate turns to me and whistles in approval.

"Damn, you look good! Going on a Nate date?" Her comment makes Kenni look at me from the couch. She's curled up under a blanket, with a bowl of quinoa in her lap and her laptop at her feet. Judging by the sounds coming from the screen, I think she's watching a courtroom drama of sorts.

"No, just dinner with my father," I say, taking the seat next to Nicole.

"Oh, that'll be fun!" says Nicole in a chipper voice. Drew shakes her head, her eyes widened, a clear indication for Nicole to stop talking. "What?"

"Ex-nay on the daddy-ay," Drew hisses. I laugh weakly.

"No, no, it's fine," I say, waving it away like it's nothing.

"Sorry," apologizes Nicole. She's clearly embarrassed.

"I'm serious! It's okay, really," I say with a smile on my face, trying to reassure her she's done nothing wrong. "Not your fault my dad is a tool." My phone buzzes in my pocket. When I click the home button, I see a text from my father. *On my way, five minutes.*

"How far away is he?" asks Kenni as if on cue.

"Five minutes." Kenni's eyes widen, and she shares a look with Drew. I can tell they're uncomfortable.

"He's coming *here*?" Kenni follows up.

"You just gotta say hi and smile, and I'll try to get him out of the door as fast as I can," I promise them.

"Is it okay if I'm here?" Nicole asks timidly.

"Yeah, it's fine! You can meet the King of Darkness," I say with a weak chuckle.

"He can't be that bad," says Nicole, trying not to sound taken aback. In the silence that follows, I get up and go to the kitchen, rummaging through the cabinet to find something small to eat. I know I'm not going to want to eat at dinner, partially due to nerves and partially because if I eat too much, I'll hear about it later when I end up eating nothing with my father. Dad will be pissed that he's going to pay for a dinner that I won't eat, but that's his problem, not mine. I find a granola bar and quickly down it.

"He's pretty bad." I consider it for a second. "Then again, I'm probably not the best daughter, but I don't know if he deserves that at this point."

"So, as you can see, they have a great relationship," Drew jokes dryly.

Knock knock.

We all freeze. The sound comes again.

Knock knock.

I smooth my blouse and put my hair behind my shoulder. No one speaks as I walk to the door and open it.

Behind the door stands my father. Measuring in at 6'1", David Tayner is one of the most imposing figures I know. Along with being tall and somewhat muscular, my dad is always in a suit. Today, he's dressed more casually, meaning he's not wearing a tie. His piercing blue eyes stare at me as his lips curl into what looks like a forced smile. No, I *know* it's forced because his eyes don't have a gleam in them. My dad opens his arms to bring me into a hug.

"Brooklyn. So good to see you," he says, embracing me. I wrap my arms around him in what could qualify as a hug.

"Hey, Dad." I pull away from him, and he walks into the apartment. Kenni, Drew, and Nicole all turn to look at him. I see Kenni put the spoon in her mouth and smile.

"Hello, Mr. Tayner," she says.

"Hello, everyone," says my father, looking around our living room at the half-dead plants and the limply hung posters and photos. The look in his eyes indicates he's trying to hide his disgust. "What an interesting home. Paying top dollar for you to live *here* of all places." In

51

hopes of distracting him from his wasted money, I gesture to my friends.

"That's Drew, and over there is Kenni. They're my roommates," I introduce, nodding to each one in turn. My father waves hello and nods to each of them. He looks at Nicole.

"And who're you?" he asks. It sounds rude, but Nicole reacts politely, seemingly unoffended.

"I'm Nicole. I'm Drew's friend from class," says Nicole.

"Ah." My dad looks back at me. The air hangs between us until I clap my hands as a concluding gesture.

"Shall we go?" I ask.

"Sure. It was nice meeting you all." *Liar.* I open the door for my dad, and he exits the apartment. Just leaving the worn apartment makes him less tense. I can see it in the way his shoulders relax as he stands proudly on the threshold. He owns everything out here in the rest of the world but wants nothing to do with the little part of the earth I call my temporary home. Once the door shuts, he puts an arm around my shoulders and holds me close. "It's so good to see you, Brook. I feel like I haven't seen you in ages."

"Yeah," I say, going down the stairs with him beside me. I look around to make sure Nate isn't around. Thankfully, he's not, but Issac is. He's walking back from the dumpster with his hands shoved in his pockets. When he sees me, he throws a smile my way and nods in greeting. I don't want to acknowledge him, so I just give a tight smile, but my father notices.

"Who's that?" he asks shortly.

"My friend, Issac," I say simply. My father nods. He doesn't want to say anything, but I can tell he's not happy that I've been hanging around boys. I've only told him about Nate in passing, and I'm not sure he entirely heard me. It's better that way.

The inside of my dad's Audi A8 is pristine, like he drove it off the lot yesterday. My dark jeans make contact with the white leather seat. I don't think the dye will rub off, but with my father, you can never be too careful. The car hums to life, and my dad backs up into the parking lot.

"So, where are we going to eat, Brook?" asks my dad as he pulls out into the street.

"What do you feel like having?" I ask him back.

"Anything. What's the best place in town?" The best place is a dive of a barbeque joint downtown that makes the best pulled pork sandwiches I've ever tasted. They have killer sweet potato fries and a side of mac and cheese that's just a touch spicy. Graffiti of customers past adorns the walls, written in Sharpie and carved with knives. Everything in there screams biker bar. I can't go there with him. Too dirty.

"Let's go to the Italian place downtown," I suggest.

"Sounds good."

We're quiet the rest of the way there.

6

"Nice place," says my father approvingly, placing a white cloth napkin on his lap and looking around at the tasteful décor that's neither Sharpie graffiti nor biker accessories. There's light jazz music playing in the background as the waiters quietly bustle around, from table to table, refilling waters and writing down orders. I feel out of place, but my dad clearly likes it by the way he settles into his chair, shoulders back and chin held high.

"So why are you in Northwich?" I ask casually, trying not to come off as rude.

"Business meeting."

"In *Northwich*, New York? Why not New York City?"

"I don't know. I didn't plan the event," says my father rudely. I decide to bite my tongue and peruse the menu. Unlike when I'm out with my friends, I don't even look at the prices. I don't feel bad for taking money from someone who hoards it.

"Hello, folks, how are you doing tonight?" asks our waiter, a peppy 20-something with a 50-watt smile. It wouldn't surprise me if he were a grad student at Resslar. "My name is Elijah, and I'll be taking care of you. Can I start you with something to drink?"

"I'll have water," I say.

"And I'll have a beer. Stella Artois, please," requests my father, pretending to be polite.

"Alright, I'll have that right over." Elijah disappears as quickly as he came.

"How's school going?" asks my dad, putting his menu down.

"It's alright. Still have my job." I couldn't sound less interested.

"Good, but I don't just want to hear about your job."

"You don't?" I ask with a skeptical look and a raised eyebrow.

"That's a large part of it, of course, but I want to hear about other things too. How's the radio station? Your social life?" I put down my menu slowly, eyeing my father.

"You really want to know?" Again, I don't mean to sound rude, but this sudden interest in my life outside of work and school is alarming.

"Yes. We haven't talked in a while, Brooklyn." He sounds sincere. "You have a boyfriend, right?"

"Thought you didn't know," I say curtly.

"You were constantly texting someone this summer when I saw you. The name I saw on your phone was Nate, I believe? How's he?" I hate my father for being as nosey as I am. Though, on second thought, maybe that's where I get it from. Deciding not to let my indignation show, I shrug.

"He's fine. He's dealing with rush right now."

"For a fraternity?" *Why did I mention rush?* "The same one you exposed last year?" His tone is tight. I search for something to say. The obvious answer is no, but the likelihood he'll buy that is slim.

"Alright, here are your drinks!" Elijah shows up in the nick of time. He places our drinks down in front of us and takes out his notepad. "Have we decided yet, or should I give you a few more minutes?"

"I'm ready. I'll have the stuffed shells please," I say, handing over my menu.

"And I'll have the veal parmesan." My dad clearly wants our waiter to leave so he can keep grilling me, and Elijah understands. He briskly takes our menus, nods politely, and flies away, leaving me alone with my dad, to my disappointment. My dad leans in. "What fraternity is your boyfriend part of, Brooklyn?"

"Delta Rho."

"That's not the one you exposed, is it?"

"No, Dad. All the guys in that one are either suspended or in jail," I say, leaning back in my chair with my arms crossed. I know I look like a stereotypical teenager, but I can't help it. My dad brings out my defensive side. It's difficult not to argue with him when he gets going, especially when it's something I'm passionate about. He runs a hand through his gelled hair, trying to decide whether to keep interrogating me or to move on to berating me. Unsurprisingly, he goes with the ladder.

"I still can't believe you did that," he says, shaking his head and looking away from me.

"Well, it's done, so ..." I trail off, looking at my lap. My father looks like he's getting more pissed the more he thinks about what I did last year. In order to calm him down as much as possible, I keep talking. "Dad, it could be a lot worse. I could be dead."

"Brooklyn, you survived, and that's fantastic, but aren't you worried they're going to come for you again?" he asks tightly. Well, *that's* a thing I didn't think he would say. My eyebrows knit together as I look up at him.

"What?"

"Those boys that I read about, the ones who went to jail ... They don't seem like the type to give up easily," my dad says.

"Okay, first of all, only *one* of them went to jail, and he was their leader. Second, the university is keeping all frats on 24-hour watch. They step out of line, even a little bit, and they're disbanded. I'm still on speaking terms with the Campus Police officers, most of whom know me by name. I have nothing to worry about," I say reassuringly.

"Whatever you need to tell yourself to sleep at night," mutters my dad. When I give him a horrified look, he raises his hands in surrender. "I'm just worried about you, Brooklyn."

"Worried about what, Dad? The fact that I have a boyfriend, the fact that I'm working only one job, or the fact that I'm not being a decent daughter?" I burst. The people at the table next to us have started to notice our argument, but I don't care. If there's one thing my father hates, it's making a scene, and I'm fortunately good at doing that.

"Keep your voice down," my father hisses, his eyes darting around at the diners who are starting to stare.

"Why do you keep harping on the SHA frat, huh? Did you *want* me to get hurt or something? Do you *want* me to have scars to show for it?" I shoot. The murmuring around me grows louder.

"What a ridiculous thing to say! I don't want to see you hurt. You're my daughter!" Now my dad is getting in on the shouting, but he never fully shouts. He just raises his voice to a louder volume, and that, in a way, is scarier than him yelling.

"So, why, huh? *Why* am I not enough for you?" There it is. The root of all of this. I know my father is disappointed in me. He wants me to work three jobs, have no social life, and be a shut-in. He would rather have me save myself for marriage and work my ass off until then. I want to shriek in his face all the things I've done to make him angry and release a string of things I know kill him to hear. But he already looks mortified, and I'm not as heartless as he is. I know this anger is a side effect of last year. My faith in my father was low before, but now, after everything, it has hit rock bottom. I take a breath to calm myself down as I look at his wrathful face.

"How *dare* you say that?" he asks in a measured tone, through his pearly white teeth. "You're *not enough* for me? Brooklyn, I am *infinitely* proud of you."

"Then why don't you act like it? You question everything I do, you never call me to congratulate me on anything, you're always short with me ... you're barely a dad." There are tears in my eyes, and I don't know how they got there. "And I don't know what I did for you to be so distant with me." Dad looks at me in shocked horror.

"Brooklyn, I love you. You're my little girl. And I'm sorry that you feel that way. I didn't realize that." My dad sounds remorseful for once in his life. The anger in his eyes is quelled for a moment. Then he turns. "But putting your life at risk for something that wasn't necessary ... That was reckless of you. And I'll be damned if I have a reckless young woman as my daughter." There's a tense silence. We're both deciding if strangling each other is socially acceptable. Judging by how we're disrupting the other customers, I don't think those around us would mind if my father and I were suddenly at each other's throats.

"I'm not reckless," I say in a whisper. "I hunt down stories, interview sources, and do what I have to in order to—"

"No, that would be journalism. Putting yourself in danger to satisfy some need inside of you is recklessness, Brooklyn. You're treating your life with such disregard that it's disturbing," my father accuses, eyes wide, biting his tongue so he won't scream. "Someone with that sort of attitude shouldn't be a journalist."

"You—"

Thank God our waiter comes back with our food. I might've cursed out my father in this classy Italian restaurant.

And God forbid David Tayner's proper daughter give her ungrateful father a piece of her mind.

^^^

"Mom, he's absolutely infuriating," I say into my phone as I stalk up the stairs to my apartment. My mother sighs on the other end.

"Why do you think we had so many problems? He's very particular about his expectations," she says. I storm into our apartment and slam the door behind me.

"You should've heard him, talking like I was some stupid kid who doesn't understand consequences. It's not like I did what I did for fun or for kicks or whatever he's thinking. Does he not get that I was *stalked* and *kidnapped? Nothing* about that was fun!" My mom is silent. I toss my keys on the table and flop down on the couch. "What?"

"Sweetheart, you know how much I disagree with your father on multiple levels, but in this case, there's a bit of truth to what he said. I'm not saying what you did wasn't honorable," Mom jumps before I can get a word in edgewise, "but your decision to continue to see the case through was a bit adventurous. The police should've been notified the moment you received those text messages."

"They bungled the case the first time around! I wasn't about to let them do that again," I defend. Mom huffs in exhaustion. This whole thing has been so much for her. All her friends and co-workers constantly ask about me and then probably wonder if I'm mentally 'all there' behind her back. As distressing as this has been for me, it's been three times worse for my mother.

"I understand, and your father was a bit out of line pushing the subject at a nice dinner. I can see how it felt a little like a trap," Mom reasons. "Just try to be safe, alright? That's all that your dad and I want for you. It's probably the only thing we actually agree on." That gets a smile out of me. The anger I feel from the evening is dissipating, so I sigh to let some of the tension out.

"I'll try. I promise," I assure her.

"I'll hold you to that," says Mom with a little humor in her tone. "I love you. Say hello to your roommates for me."

"I will. Love you too." I hang up and let the phone fall out of my hand and on the couch beside me. As I stare at the ceiling, I realize that I don't want to see my father again for a long time. He had a point, but he will never be right. I won't let a man who calls himself my father dictate what I can and can't do with my life.

After the call ends, I realize my apartment is silent. In fact, the silence is creeping me out. I walk to my room and put my purse down on my bed. *Where is everyone?*

"Hello?" I ask. There's no response.

I leave out of the front door, walk three feet across the landing, and open the door of Finn's apartment. The rooms are arranged identical to Nate's, so when I walk into the living room, their backs are facing me. When I shut the door, Drew, Kenni, and Finn turn around. Drew's face is streaked with tears, her eyeliner running down her face. Finn has his arm around her, and Kenni is standing on Finn's other side, hugging herself like she's freezing even though the apartment is 76 degrees. Drew fully turns around, so Finn has to take his arm off her.

"Where have you been for so long?" she asks.

"At dinner with my dad. Why?" I say.

"Nicole didn't come home tonight," Finn tells me in a grim voice.

"What?" I breathe. Kenni stays silent like she's afraid to speak.

"No one knows where she went," continues Finn.

"She was walking home from our apartment, Brook," Drew whispers. "*Our* apartment ..." She bursts into tears again. It scares me to see her this broken, but it scares me more to wonder why Nicole didn't make it home.

On this exact day.

At this exact time.

While I was gone.

I don't want to jump to conclusions or seem paranoid. But I know enough to realize this cannot possibly be a coincidence.

Vengeance

Drew's sobs clog my ears as I stare at the ground in a trance, the churning in my stomach just growing and growing.

7

"And she said she was going straight home?" I reiterate, pacing around our living room. The little gathering has moved back to our house with Drew and Finn on the couch and Kenni sitting at the table. Finn thought Drew might be more comfortable in her own apartment. His arm is around her as she's curled up next to him. Every once in a while, she wipes a tear from her face. She's thinking the same thing I am: My curse has extended to my friends.

"Yeah, she said she was going back to her apartment. She's a junior. She lives off-campus," Drew says, still shaking in horror. I nod and bite my fingernail, looking at the ground. I stay quiet for a bit. "Brooklyn, say something!"

"What do you want me to say, Drew?" I burst, stopping my pacing and facing her. "I'm just as lost as you are."

"She wouldn't have run away, right?" Kenni asks.

"She loves Resslar. Why would she just up and leave?" Drew replies.

"I don't know. She's your friend!" Kenni says defensively.

"Okay, calm down. We're all shaken up. Let Brooklyn think," says Finn. I glare at him with narrowed eyes.

"Why aren't *you* guys thinking?" I spit, my anger a side effect of the evening's events. Finn shakes his head, realizing how ignorant his comment sounded.

"Brook, I didn't mean—"

"Just because I was a detective *one time* doesn't mean I'm willing to go through this again! That SHA shit was *hell*, and I just *barely* came out alive," I say with disbelief at Finn. Once I realize my tone, my head shakes a bit. "Sorry, I'm just scared." After taking a measured breath through my nose, I look at Drew again. Her tears are drying on her face. "Drew, she's your friend. Can you think of any reason she wouldn't come home? Boyfriend, job, anything?"

"No," Drew breathes. "Besides you guys, she's my best friend. If she wanted to leave, she'd tell me."

"Did she have any enemies that you're aware of?" I ask.

"No," Drew says.

"Anyone who would benefit in some way from having her gone?"

"No."

"Anyone who could *possibly* have it out for her?"

"No!"

"Drew, I need you to think!" I explode.

"I AM THINKING!" she shrieks.

BANG BANG.

The living room falls silent. We seem to collectively tense up at the loudness of the sound.

BANG BANG.

"Let me in!" comes Nate's muffled voice. I let go of a breath I didn't know I was holding and unlock the front door. The lock clicks, and I open the door to my frigid boyfriend. I look over his sweaty mess of a body as I shut the door. He's wearing a sweatshirt, t-shirt, shorts, and sneakers, a totally inappropriate outfit for the cold windy weather outside.

"What's with the shorts?" I question.

"Just came from the gym and thought I would drop by." He takes a look around the living room, sees Finn consoling Drew, sees Kenni with a worried expression, and raises an eyebrow. "Clearly I came at the wrong time. What's up?"

"Drew's friend, Nicole, went missing," Kenni explains.

"The girl in the CP email? You know her?" Nate asks in shock.

"They sent an email?" Finn replies.

"Yeah, just to let us know to be on the lookout for her. Also told us to not go anywhere alone at night. Got it while I was running." Nate looks at me. "You don't think ..."

"Nothing in the case indicates this was a frat's doing," I try to reassure him, although I don't know how confident I sound. "I don't think it could be anyone close to Taylor, but it could be someone else who has it out for the university. Or a copycat of some sort," I add after a second. Nate scoffs, a proud smile on his face.

"Knew you'd get back in the game at one point." He sits down in the chair opposite Kenni at the table. I see her try to stifle a smile out of agreement.

"I'm not *back in the game*," I say, pushing my hair away from my face.

"Not right now, but you won't be able to stay away for long. You crave this kind of shit," Nate says. He looks at Drew. "You knew her, huh?"

"Yeah. She was a really good friend. She was walking home from this apartment when it happened." Nate's face falls.

"Oh, no one said anything about *that* bit."

"Yeah," Drew says shortly.

"How can they call her officially missing if she hasn't been gone for 24 hours? Isn't that a thing?" Nate asks.

"Her roommates must've been jarred too. They know her schedule better than I do," Drew reasons.

"Look, it's no use worrying about her now. I say we try to get some sleep," Finn suggests.

"I have a huge test tomorrow. I should study," Kenni says, sounding almost ashamed. "If you want to over-analyze this, Brook, you can. I would just say to not look too far into things. I'm sure she just took a different route home or something." She stands up and stretches her arms above her head. "Night, everyone." There's a chorus of us saying goodnight to her as she walks down the hallway to her room. Nate looks back at Drew.

"I'm sorry, Drew. CP or the cops will find her tomorrow. I'm sure of it." Drew nods, clearly appreciating the sympathy.

"You want me to stay here tonight?" Finn asks her.

"You won't mind?" she asks.

"Tomorrow's Sunday. What do I have to get up for?" Finn kisses her on the head and gets off the couch. "I'm gonna get a shirt from my apartment. Give me two minutes. I'll be right back." Finn waves goodbye to me and Nate, opens the door, letting in a huge gust of frosty air, and then shuts it behind him.

"Hey, how was dinner with your dad?" Nate asks me.

"Infuriating, but I survived. How was the gym?"

"Difficult, but I survived." I smile at him. He takes my hand and squeezes reassuringly. "Hey, seriously, don't jump to anything, alright? You've done enough in terms of university mysteries as it is. They'll find her." Nate stands and kisses me on the cheek. "I gotta go shower. I love you."

"Love you too," I say distracted, giving him a peck on the lips before he leaves. Finn comes back into the living room, and I lock the door behind him. I start towards my room, but something makes me pause and turn around. "Hey, Drew?"

"Hm?" Her eyes are wide and hopeful as they look at me.

"She's out there somewhere. I promise." Drew smiles thankfully at me, then walks with Finn into her room.

Once I enter my room and trudge to my bed, I change into my pajamas. I'm ready to sleep and forget this day ever happened. It takes two makeup wipes to take off my mask of foundation, mascara, and eyeliner, but when it is off, my skin feels like it can breathe. I sit down at my desk and open my laptop, checking my email one more time to make sure no one from WRDW has any emergencies. My hand rests on the desk on the side of my laptop and my fingers wrap around a USB—

Wait.

I stare at the USB on my desk. It sits there, its black casing gleaming.

I haven't used a USB since the fifth grade.

What the hell is this doing here?

Out of curiosity, I uncap the USB and plug it into the side of my laptop. When my computer processes it, a folder pops up. There's only one video file in it. I gulp and look around to confirm I'm alone, then click it.

I hold back a scream.

A person in a black hood and a *V is for Vendetta* mask pops up on the screen. His hoodie perfectly blends into the black background, so he looks like a disembodied head. I'm paralyzed when he starts to talk in a clearly altered deep voice.

"Hello, Brooklyn Perce. By now, you've heard about the disappearance of Nicole Walters. She is in my care now. She is the first but will not be the last." I'm paralyzed by fear, wishing I could tear my eyes away from the screen. The man continues. "You must pay for what you've done, Brooklyn. You need to learn your actions have consequences. So, if you do not find the students that I will take, I will kill them."

"Holy shit," I breathe, my gaze still fixated on the screen. *My dad was right.* I squeeze my eyes shut and open them, but it's not a nightmare. The video is still playing.

"It will be fun taking them. It will be a game for me. I will take one at a time until you remain, and only then will I finally kill you."

"Oh my God," I whisper, tears welling in my eyes.

"Come find the ones I take, and you and the others will be spared. Don't, and they die. I look forward to killing you, Brooklyn Perce."

The video stops, and I just sit in deafening silence.

8

My knees hit the wooden floor of the fraternity house. There's a hand on the back of my neck forcing me down, but I can't see who it is. As I fight the pressure growing on my spine, I glance upward. Taylor is holding a paddle adorned with the SHA Greek letters and is staring down at me with maniacal glee.

"You deserve this," he says in a monotone. That's when he starts hitting me. The paddle whacks me across the face, knocking out some of my teeth and causing my mouth to bleed. The next hit comes from the other side and breaks my nose. I scream in pain as my nose starts to bleed. Taylor hits me in the side with the paddle, breaking at least two of my ribs. The men behind me don't even have to hold me down anymore; I've become a crumpled mess on the floor. That's when Taylor steps aside and reveals Mask Man standing behind him.

"I look forward to killing you, Brooklyn Perce," he says from behind the mask in a robotic voice. He puts his foot on the side of my head and slowly presses down until my skull cracks under the pressure.

When I wake up the next morning, my body automatically sits up straight in bed, and my eyes search the room. No one in a mask is here.

Trudging into the kitchen, I first smell eggs frying in a pan and then see Finn cooking them at the stove. He looks well-rested, something I envy him for. The inside of my mouth is dry as I hear the quiet crackling of the yolks. I rub my eyes and yawn. Finn notices my haggard appearance and raises an eyebrow.

"Couldn't sleep?" he asks.

"No," I say curtly, opening the fridge and pulling out the jug of milk. Finn sees what I'm doing and pipes up again.

"Oh, I'm making—"

"Thanks, but I'm not very hungry to be honest," I say, trying not to sound ungrateful.

"Alright, you're missing out though," says Finn. I know I should eat something substantial before I try to figure out the Mask Man's identity, but I can't bring myself to do it. Whatever I eat, I might just vomit back up. I pour myself a glass of milk and down it in a gulp until the dry feeling is satiated.

"Is Drew okay?" I ask kindly, trying to make up for being rude before.

"She's still shaken up, but she'll be fine. We're going to the mall today to take her mind off of things," Finn tells me.

"Are you buying her—?"

"Chipotle? Of course." I smile at him. He knows Drew too well. Out of the corner of my eye, I see him give me a once-over. "Are you sure you're okay?"

"Yeah. I just didn't get enough sleep, that's all," I say nonchalantly, brushing it off.

"You just seem … not like yourself." I know he's prying out of love, but I'm not in the mood for his sympathy.

"I'm going to Nate's," I decide aloud. Once I put the milk jug back in the fridge, I go into my room and change out of my PJs into leggings, a large sweater, and tall boots. I snatch my laptop from my desk and throw it into my backpack. I also pocket the USB after deciding it's not smart to leave it out in the open. Finn nods to me as I leave.

"Oh, Brook! Want me to get you anything from Chipotle?" he asks, still being his nice perky self. I smile thankfully.

"Some chips and guacamole would be amazing," I say. Finn gives me a thumbs up.

"Tell Nate I say hi," he requests. I flash him a smile, then open the front door and leave.

The chilly November air hits my face as I make the three-second walk over to Nate's apartment. When I open the door to his apartment, the warm air engulfs me. When I put down my backpack on the kitchen table, I see Nate's third roommate, Kienan, sitting there with a girl. She has brown hair that falls in a perfectly straight waterfall down her back. The tips of her long mane are dyed a navy blue, so they stand out from the grey sweatshirt she's wearing. When she turns to look at me, I see she has innocent-looking sapphire eyes. She smiles as though she's forcing herself to be friendly. Clearly, I've interrupted a conversation.

"Kienan, you didn't tell me you had the campus celebrity as a friend," she says with a tinge of mocking in her voice. I feel prickles forming on my skin out of irritation, a sensation that's familiar nowadays.

"She's Nate's girlfriend. Brooklyn, this is Jordyn," Kienan introduces. I give her the best strained smile I can muster.

"Nice to meet you," I say.

"Oh, so you're *Nathan's*?" Jordyn asks. A small, infuriating, unimpressed snort escapes her. "I must say, he knows how to pick 'em." I sneer at her as she flashes me a syrupy smile, clearly happy to be getting under my skin.

"Heard my name?" My boyfriend comes out of his room, running a hand through his hair in an attempt to make himself look presentable. He clearly just got out of bed as indicated by his frumpy RU logo sweats and lack of a shirt. I walk over to him and look him in the eyes urgently. His tiredness seems to vanish when he understands my expression.

"I need to talk to you ... alone," I add. Jordyn is surveying Nate's bare upper body with hungry eyes. My stomach twists and turns, wanting to cave in on itself as I see the way she's looking at him.

"Good *morning*, Nathan," says Jordyn like a fox about to kill its prey. "Had a nice night?"

"Yeah," says Nate, giving her a wary glance. I know he's uncomfortable with her looking at him the way she does. It's good to know my feelings are shared. He turns to me. "I'm gonna splash some water on my face, but you can go to my room. I'll be there soon." Nate glances one last time at Jordyn and walks down the hall to the bathroom.

"Talk to you later, Brook," says Kienan in his loud voice. After I give him a half-hearted wave, I excuse myself and enter Nate's room.

Inside, I see the sneakers he was wearing last night on the floor, kicked to a corner along with his socks from yesterday. There's a little bit of an odor to his room that I can't decide whether I like or not. I rearrange the bedspread so I can sit on it, and in comes Nate. He widens his eyes and shuts the door.

"Sorry about her. She's Kienan's friend. She's always over here," he apologizes.

"Where'd she come from?" I say in a lowered voice just in case Jordyn also has wandering ears.

"She's a sophomore, and Kienan's sweet on her for some reason. I think she's in a class or two of his or something." Nate sits in his desk chair like he did the other day. He notices how quiet I am as I process the information. "What?"

"Nothing. It's nothing. There are more important things I have to talk to you about." Nate raises an eyebrow as I unload my laptop and pull out the USB. "I found this last night." He stares at it and then looks at me skeptically.

"*Found*?" he repeats.

"It was on my desk."

"Okay, so?" He's still not getting it.

"*So*, I've never used a USB in college. Ever." I shove the storage device into the USB drive of my computer as Nate tentatively gets up and comes to my side. Once the USB icon pops up on my desktop, I click on the folder.

My face falls.

"It's gone," I say, troubled by the disappearance. Nate blankly stares at the empty screen in front of us.

"What's gone?" My finger frantically taps the trackpad of my computer, closing and then re-opening the device. Still not there.

"The-the-the video! It's not there!" I madly close and reopen the USB five times in a row, but there's still nothing. I thrust my hands in my hair, staring at my laptop in disbelief. I turn to Nate. "There was a video of a guy in a mask, one of those creepy *V for Vendetta* ones, and-and he was telling me he took Nicole! He said he was gonna take every last person on this campus until I pay for exposing the fraternity!" I speak in such a mad rush that when I'm done, Nate looks at me like I've lost it. I huff. "You don't believe me."

"Brooklyn, when did you find the video?" he asks me levelly. I shut the laptop and put it on his bed, springing up and facing him with my arms crossed. "I'm just asking when did you see it?"

"Last night before I went to bed."

"Okay, so it could've been a dream."

"I know what I saw, Nate!" I exclaim, "I'm not lying!"

"Brook, there's no video there. In theory, you could've dreamt it." I look at him incredulously, and he puts his hands up in surrender. "Babe, I'm not saying you're lying, but what if you dreamt this?"

"Nate. Why would I make this up?" I say, trying not to yell for the sake of Kienan and his friend outside. "There was a man in a mask telling me he kidnapped Nicole and he'll kidnap everyone at this school if he has to, until I'm the only one left, and then he's gonna kill me." Nate's eyes widen. "Oh, so now you believe me?"

"Woah! Woah! He threatened to *kill* you?" Nate's talking in a hushed voice now. "You didn't mention that before."

"Everything I *do* at Resslar comes with a death threat. I thought I didn't have to *mention it!*" I say sarcastically. Nate gets up from the bed and looks down at me, worry forming in his eyes.

"Try to remember what he said word for word," he says, a slight tremor in his voice.

"Something about how he took Nicole and she's the first but won't be the last. There was a part in there about how if I don't find the people he's somehow taking, he's going to kill them." Now, he's scared.

"This man said he's going to *murder* the people he takes?" Nate asks. I nod. "All of them?" I nod again. Nate seems fed up with himself, as though he thinks he should know better by now. "Right, no witnesses." It's not that he doesn't believe *me*. It's that he doesn't want to believe *this*. I don't want to either. "You gonna go to the cops?" he asks after a second of silence.

"I was gonna go to Greenwood tomorrow. Conveniently, today is his day off." Nate nods and runs his hand over his face like a worried father. Meanwhile, my eyes have been studying a spot on his desk just above a drawer handle. I'm slowly realizing what has to happen. "I don't want to go through this again," I whisper, tears welling in my eyes. "The nightmares still haven't ..." Nate puts his hands on my shoulders. This snaps me out of my trance, and I don't get a chance to look up at him before he embraces me.

"I know, Brook. I know ..." I bury my face in his chest. "It's okay." We stand there for a moment, him engulfing me and me taking him in. I live for moments like this when the world stands still, and it's just me and the best man on the planet. I wish I could bottle this feeling of comfort and save it for moments when he's not there, for moments like yesterday's dinner, for moments when I've woken up in the middle of the night because I've been battling monsters in my dream.

Then I realize I'm being stupid.

Why break down? It gets me nowhere and does me no favors. The more time I waste in here, the more time Mask Man is out there. I bite back a bitter laugh when I realize my dad would want me to quit right now and let qualified people handle things. I don't think I can ever be that person. Someone wants me and those around me dead. I can't in good conscience step away from this entirely. I won't.

I break the hug and swiftly wipe off the tear falling from my left eye with a fingertip. Nate notices my sudden change of heart and doesn't seem too keen on it. He looks more and more confused by the second, but I'm used to my sudden mood reversals by now. He furrows his brow as I look at him with conviction.

"What are you thinking about?" he asks.

"I'm gonna find him," I tell him solemnly. After a moment's hesitation, Nate nods in agreement.

"Alright. So, let's find him."

9

"Brooklyn Perce here to see Roger Greenwood."
When I enter the Campus Police office the next day, the
receptionist looks me up and down before typing
something into her computer. She knows me by now,
and I know her: Hallie Stewart, late 30s, planning on
traveling the world once she retires. Yes, she has her
retirement planned out already. I suspect a lot of adults
who work here do.

"Ah, yes, I see you're in the schedule, Ms. Perce. Have
a seat," Hallie says. I go to sit down, but before I can
even move, there's a groan from above.

"Oh, God." Both Hallie and I glance at the top of the
stairs where I see Campus Police Officer Roger
Greenwood looking as young and smug as ever. The
officer and I didn't see eye to eye last year, and this year
is no different. After the work Greenwood did last year,
his boss thought the rookie cop could keep me out of
trouble. Although, at the time, Greenwood acted like he
appreciated the promotion, he despised watching over
me like a parent, a feeling that hasn't changed. The

feeling is mutual. He looks down at me from the high landing and raises his eyebrows skeptically. "This'll be good."

I walk up the stairs and shut his office door behind me as I enter. Adorning the walls of his massive room are paintings of various landscapes, mixed with awards that I'm sure are all irrelevant now. Greenwood sits behind his desk and leans back in his chair, eyeing me doubtingly.

"Hello, Officer," I say, sitting up so straight that my back hurts.

"Hello. So, what's troubling you today?" He's trying not to sound cynical and failing miserably.

"I received a video on this USB two nights ago." I put the USB down on the table. He looks at it and then at me, unimpressed. "In the video, there was a person in a mask telling me he kidnapped Nicole Walters, and then said he'd kidnap everyone on this campus, if necessary, to teach me a lesson." Greenwood raises his eyebrows. He doesn't seem like he believes me. I don't blame him.

"Where'd you find the USB?" he finally says.

"In my mailbox," I smoothly lie, thinking that's a better answer than trying to explain how Mask Man got into my locked apartment. Heaving a deep breath, Greenwood leans forward, hand outstretched to take the memory stick.

"Well, let's pull the video up then," he grunts as though this is taking him the maximum amount of effort.

"It's not on the USB anymore." Greenwood scoffs. "I'm serious. I opened it once, and then, when I tried to open it again, it was gone. It self-destructed or something." As he tries to piece together the puzzle, he leans back into his chair again.

"You're telling me that someone threatened the campus via a video file, saying they were doing it to teach you a lesson, but you can't show me the video because it ... *self-destructed*." He looks at me like I must be kidding. All I can do is shrug.

"I know it sounds stupid, but this is part of the deal that I made with—"

"Yes, yes, I know. Complete transparency with us after last year's stunt," he waves away. He pauses. "He didn't make a threat on your life? Just wanted to teach you a lesson?" *Transparency.* That's an interesting word for him to use.

"No, he didn't say he'd come after me."

"Just wants to isolate you?" I nod again. Greenwood heaves another dramatic sigh. It's clear he wishes he had better things to do than hunt down a man in a mask, but, sadly, protecting the community is part of the job. He pinches the bridge of his nose. "Jesus, Perce."

"All of the campus's problems would be solved if I just transferred," I weakly joke. Greenwood snorts.

"You'd never get into another college. They wouldn't want the trouble that comes with you," Greenwood says, finally cracking a faint smile. He fully leans forward, folding his hands on his desk. "Alright, leave the USB with me, and I'll see if we can get someone from IT to retrieve the video. If it's a kid threatening you, I doubt he or she covered their tracks well. We'll send out an email, in addition to the one about Nicole just to be on the lookout for any suspicious figures or activity, and I'll talk to my boss about seeing if the Chancellor will institute a curfew. She's usually good with that sort of thing." He notices how I'm staying quiet. "Any problems with that plan?"

"No, I think you covered it," I say, getting up and putting my backpack over my shoulder. "Let me know if you retrieve the video. I need to get to the radio station."

"Alright, thanks for letting us know." I start to leave. "Oh, Brooklyn?" I stop and turn around. "Stay out of this. I'm serious. Do *not* pry." I give him an innocent smile.

"Why would I want to put myself through that again?" I ask in a sweet voice. Greenwood smirks. "Bye, Officer." I leave the office and shut the door behind me.

^^^

I sit down in an editing booth at WRDW with the usual folder of ready-for-air stories on the desk beside me. Part of my job is reviewing the news stories students have written and tweaking the leads or the wording slightly to make them more appealing to the listener. I'm just getting in the zone when I hear a knock on the door frame of the little room.

"Hey, Brooklyn," says Conor, smiling. His light green eyes are accented by the pale blue quarter zip he's wearing over a white t-shirt. The tan pants on his legs are nicely pressed. He looks at me, with his left eyebrow slightly raised. "Reporting for duty."

"Good." Heading for the larger newsroom, I try to edge by him to leave the suite. He makes it hard for me to get around him, but a swift look of annoyance from me puts him in his place. "You're working today on the audio that Julie collected over the weekend at an event for the mayoral race. It's regarding the fall out. Northwich hasn't had a Green Party candidate win in years. Transcribe it, pull sound bites, the whole thing. Think you can handle that?" Conor nods and examines my face, his eyes scanning my features as though he's trying to find something. "What are you doing?"

"You look preoccupied. What happened this weekend with Dad, Brooklyn?" he asks in a soft, sly voice. The right corner of his mouth curves up in a sneer.

It takes a lot of self-restraint not to angrily slam him against the wall he's leaning on.

"Mind your own business, Valree," I say through my teeth. "Get to work."

"You're pretty, Brooklyn, but you're gorgeous when you're in distress," Conor says. *That's it.* If it's witty banter he wants, it's witty banter he'll get. I saunter back over to him, making eye contact the whole way. The haughty look on his face slips slightly, but he still looks like he could own the entire world. I stop in front of him, my fingers itching to clench into fists at my sides. Conor suddenly looks like he doesn't want to play the game he started.

"You must think you're amazing, Conor. You've been treated like the privileged little boy you are for your entire life. I'm sure you've gotten away with a lot of shit most people wouldn't dream of." Conor's cocky look has frozen on his face. I continue, relishing stunning him. "But I'm not a pushover, and I'm not flattered easily. As long as you're in this building, you *will* treat me with respect *as your boss*. I'm not some girl you're picking up at a frat party, Conor. I'm the goddamn student manager of this station, and if you won't treat me as such, I swear to God your career in radio will end before it even begins."

With one last threatening look, I turn on my heel and go back into my editing booth, ready to cut sound.

^^^

I sit through class and then find a chair at Newsworthy Café to do some homework. Conor's comment has rolled over in my mind this entire day. That smug boy is more trouble than he's worth. I would go to Peter about him, but my manager would think that's childish, and it is. Complaining to someone about a person who's annoying me and not taking matters into my own hands is what a first grader would do. I'll handle him on my own.

My laptop opens, and my email loads. Unsurprisingly, there's nothing from Greenwood yet. I slump in my seat, trying to hold back my impatience. The cops around here are too slow. While they dawdle, Nicole is rotting somewhere.

"Hey," says a somewhat familiar voice. I glance up from my computer and see the boy from Fraanco. His grey eyes smile at me. "I remember you."

"Yeah," I say, trying to push past my uncomfortable feeling and act politely. "Gavin, right?"

"You got it." He gestures to the chair across the table from me. "Mind if I sit?" *Yes, I absolutely do.* I just smile in response, and he takes that as a cue to sit down. His long legs settle in underneath the table, and he pulls out his laptop. The jittery fear that I experienced earlier is back, creeping up from my toes, invading my whole body. "I'm swamped with homework. Fraanco loves throwing work at me. Well, you know, you're a marketing minor if I remember correctly."

"Yeah, they still have to accept me, but that's the plan. Which classes are killing you?" I ask absentmindedly, making polite conversation but reading up on the latest local news to distract myself from the creeping wave of uneasiness. Nicole's disappearance is already on the third page. The news cycle is ruthless.

"My basic accounting class and my intro to economics class. They suck." Gavin types something into his computer and clicks around. "Hey, did you see the email about the girl who was kidnapped?"

"Yeah. Scary, huh?" I say. *Can you stop talking and do your damn work?*

"Very. The cops are on it, though. I trust them." I feel like telling him that he shouldn't, but I don't want to kill the freshman's hope just yet. "Does this kind of shit happen often around here? Underground frats, people disappearing?"

"Never a dull moment, that's for sure," I say with a little smile I hope he can't tell is forced.

"And you're ... what? Nancy Drew?" Gavin asks with a little chuckle. I consider it.

"Something like that." The two of us laugh a little at the absurdity of it. When I force myself to look at him, I notice a bit of blue in his eyes that stands out with the sunlight shining in through the window. The blue is a sort of navy, not seafoam, and it compliments his face nicely. Gavin looks at me admiringly, and my forced smile grows. The way his eyes bore into mine still makes my intestines twist and cave in on themselves. This is how I know the fear has crept up to my stomach.

"Hey, you!" I look to my left and see Nate approaching. Now, my smile turns into relief as he leans down and kisses me on the cheek. I see Gavin look back towards his computer sheepishly. The fear boiling in my stomach subsides when Nate sits down. "How's it going?"

"Good! Where are you coming from?"

"BDJ230. It was tough today, but it's super interesting. I'm really getting into it." Nate looks across the table to Gavin, who's sitting up straight but looks like he wants to shrink. "And who're you?"

"Gavin Wryte," he pipes up, shaking Nate's hand.

"Nate Stevenson," says Nate, staring at him with wary eyes. "Where'd you meet Brook?"

"I was at Fraanco doing stuff for my minor, and I sat next to him," I say. Nate nods.

"Nice to meet you." Nate pulls out the seat to my left and plops down. He seems exhausted. He runs a hand through his brown hair and then looks at me as if to say *Did you go to Greenwood?* I get his silent message loud and clear and nod in response.

"Gavin!" *That's* a voice I never wanted to hear again. Jordyn comes over to the table with her mouth open in mock surprise. She's wearing a tight top, leggings, and heeled boots, an outfit that won't keep her warm one bit on a day like today. "Fancy seeing you here!" Nate gulps as he fixes his hair. I want to ask him why he's suddenly so red.

"Hey, Jordyn!" exclaims Gavin, relieved not to be third wheeling anymore. "Guys, this is—"

"We've met," I say through a fake smile. "Nice seeing you."

"Hey," she smacks. Jordyn gasps a bit when she sees Nate. "Oh, look who it is!" She walks over to him, and even in the three steps she takes, it looks like she's walking down a runway. "If it's not my favorite resident of Kienan's apartment."

"Hey, Jordyn," says Nate, nodding politely and putting on a grin that I can see through instantly. She stands over him and puts her hands on his shoulders. I see him tense up. She looks at the top of his head like it's the sexiest thing she's ever seen.

"How do you and Gavin know each other?" I ask loudly. Jordyn's eyes collide with mine, and I give her a death glare. Her hands are still on Nate, the acrylic nails on her fingertips hooking around his shoulders like talons.

"We live on the same floor," Gavin says, looking at Nate with slight envy.

"Yes, Gavin's very social," says Jordyn. She seems like she's suddenly been reminded of the other good-looking guy sitting next to my boyfriend. Even though Gavin catches her eyes, she's still focused on Nate. She taps him lightly on the shoulders with both hands. Nate slightly winces. "How lucky I am! I'm headed over to Kienan's now. I'll get to see you twice in one day."

"Great," says Nate in a deadpan.

"What class did you get out of?" Gavin asks.

"COM107. I just transferred to Rosenburg, so I have to take freshmen lectures," she says, sounding like she'd rather be watching paint dry.

"Oh, that's where I met Brook!" says Nate, leaning forward on the table to make her release him from her hold. Jordyn simpers.

"Aw, how lovely. So cute." She stares daggers at my prideful face. Our staring contest ends when I make fists with my hands, one of which sits on top of the table. That's when she realizes she's no longer welcome. "I'm going to go catch the bus. Great seeing you all. Ciao."

She twiddles her fingers, flips her hair over her shoulder, and leaves. I see Nate deflate a bit as he puts his hand through his hair, trying to correct its style that was somewhat ruined by Jordyn.

"She's something, huh?" Gavin says like he's coming out of a trance.

"Yeah, she's great," I respond in a flat tone. Gavin shakes his head.

"She's friends with a lot of guys."

"Really?" I say, looking at Nate who grimaces.

"Well, I wouldn't call them *friends*, actually. More like *collectibles*."

"Collectibles?" I repeat, raising an eyebrow. Gavin nods.

"I know it sounds weird, but you never know where you stand with her. She's always a mystery." He looks at me. "But you know what that's like, right, Nancy Drew?" I scoff and look at him, still trying to figure him out. Out of the corner of my eye, I see Nate's eyebrows crease as he looks between us. Gavin looks at me the way he looked at Jordyn.

"Sadly, I do."

10

"You ever wonder if you see the same colors as other people?" That's the conversation I walk into as I enter my apartment. I lean my back against the front door and see Kenni chomp thoughtfully down on a green bean.

"I can't say I have," says Kenni to Drew. She smiles at me and waves.

"Like, *I* know blue is blue, but what if you've been told that purple is called blue?" Drew pokes her head out of the kitchen and notices there's something wrong. "What's up, Brook?"

"I just ... I think a freshman flirted with me. *In front* of Nate," I say. Kenni's eyes widen.

"Damn, who's the guy?"

"This kid I met in Fraanco when I was signing up for my minor. Gavin Wryte," I say, putting my bag on the floor.

"What did he do?"

"We just talked, but he called me Nancy Drew and just stared into my eyes ..." His entrancing stare pops into my mind, and I feel a chill run through me. "It was unsettling."

"Did Nate say anything?" Drew asks.

"No, but I could tell he noticed. I didn't say anything when Jordyn hit on him in front of me," I exclaim.

"Jordyn?" Drew asks, over-pronouncing the name as though the sounds are unnatural.

"Pretty, tall, flirt," I groan. "She's aggravating." I drop down into the uncomfortable chair at the kitchen table across from Kenni and take a string bean, chewing it thoughtfully.

"You're pretty and tall!" says Kenni, reproachfully.

"I'm like five foot six on a good day. She's got these long legs." I put my head in my hands. "She's gorgeous."

"Well, did Nate look like he was enjoying it?" asks Drew.

"He looked uncomfortable but didn't tell her to stop," I say. "He, like, fixed his hair and got red when she came up to us." Kenni's face falls. "What?"

"Yikes," she says in a low voice.

"But when the freshman was flirting with you, did you tell him to stop?" Drew chirps. I fall silent and chew on my bottom lip. "Brook ... Tell me you told him to shut up." I look at the table and Drew groans. "Brooklyn!"

"Nate came and broke it up!" I defend.

"Was that before or after you sunk into the freshman's eyes?" retorts Drew.

"I just *looked* at him, Drew. It's not like I'm gonna sleep with him or something!" The room goes silent. Drew and Kenni are exchanging judgmental looks as I just sit at the table and stare at the last green bean on Kenni's plate. "The way she looked at him ... made me sick."

"You're not one for being quiet, Brooklyn. So, what made you shut up?" she asks.

"His response to her. Just her presence cast a sort of spell on him."

"Spoken like a true journalist," Kenni murmurs.

"I don't wanna talk about this anymore." My back hits the back of the chair. "I'll deal with Nate later. How was class without Nicole, Drew?"

"Horrible. Our professor basically told us that we need to watch our backs because any of us could be next. Uplifting message," she says sarcastically.

"Sounds like it," I say.

"He's right, though. We could get kidnapped at any point," Kenni points out.

"Not as long as I'm going after him," I say in a final way, standing up and taking Kenni's last green bean. I walk to the couch and plop down, taking out my laptop from my backpack to do some work. Scrolling through my emails, I see nothing new from Greenwood. Figures.

Ring ring. Ring ring.

It's an unknown number. Against my better judgement, I pick up.

"Hello?"

"Hey, Brook! I was going through Nate's room, looking for something of mine, and I found a shirt you left here. Want me to bring it over?" asks Issac in a peppy voice.

"Hey, Issac," I say in a relieved tone.

"You good?" he asks.

"Yeah, I'm fine! Sure, you can bring it over. I actually have his sweatshirt to give back to him. Do you want me to come over instead? I mean, it's my stuff."

"No, I'll come to your place! I want out of this house for a bit. I'll see you in two seconds." He hangs up, and I hear Kenni starting to wash her dinner dishes. Drew is sitting at the kitchen table, picking at the pasta she made herself. When she tastes a piece, she makes a face.

"I can never get a perfect al dente," Drew grumbles.

"Who are you waitin' for?" Kenni asks me over the sound of water hitting dishes.

"Issac," I say. Kenni drops whatever bowl she was washing, walks out of the kitchen with her dishwashing gloves dripping on the floor, and looks at me with wide eyes.

"Why didn't you tell me?! I gotta go get ready!" she says, gesturing to her outfit of sweatshirt and leggings.

"Those leggings make your butt look good. You're fine," Drew waves away, taking a timid bite of a curly piece of pasta. Kenni awkwardly throws her hair over her shoulder and looks towards the door as she hears me open it. In comes Issac, who smiles at me and nods.

"Hey," I say.

"Hey, Brook. Hey, Drew." He looks at the kitchen and smiles. "Hey, Kenni."

"Issac, is that you? Hey!" Kenni calls as though she was totally thrown off guard. She waves her gloved hand, and he waves back.

"Have my shirt?" I ask him.

"Yep." He hands over the red blouse I was wearing a few days ago. "Have the sweatshirt?"

"Yeah. Actually, come with me. I gotta get it from my closet." Issac follows me down the hall, and I see

Kenni crane her neck to watch Issac leave. Issac turns back, and Kenni sheepishly looks down at the sink.

I chuck the shirt he gave me into my laundry bag when I enter my room. Issac looks around and nods approvingly as I open the closet and give him the sweatshirt.

"That's for Nate. And thanks for running that over here," I say, nodding to the laundry bag in the corner.

"Yeah, no problem! Figured you want it back." He looks at my desk, and his eyebrows crease. "Looks like you have Drew's beanie too."

"What?" I glance to my desk, and my stomach drops. On the pristine surface is a green beanie that I don't own.

But I know who it belongs to.

I make a sudden move towards the door. Issac quickly hustles out of my room, not understanding why I'm suddenly hurrying. Once he's gone, I go over to my desk and snatch the green thing. After I ball it up in my fist, I bring the beanie into the kitchen.

"Brook, is everything okay?" Issac asks. Drew looks up from the table, clearly perturbed by my jumpy manner.

"Yeah," I say tightly. Kenni pokes her head out of the kitchen again.

"What's up?" she asks. I look at her with eyes that tell her to shut up, but she doesn't get the hint. Kenni nods to my hand. "What're you holding?"

"Is this yours?" I ask Drew, throwing the beanie on the table. She looks at it, considers it for a second, then shakes her head.

"I don't own any green beanies," she says.

"Shit," I breathe.

"Do you want me to leave?" Issac asks, unsure of what's happening. I do need him to leave, but I can't be rude. Slowly turning to him, I plaster on a smile.

"I'm sorry. I sort of freaked out, Issac. I'm still a bit jumpy from last year's, you know, ... *incident*," I say. "Everything's alright." Issac only halfway takes the bait, giving me a confused smile.

"Okay, you sure you're fine?"

"Perfect. Tell Nate I say hi," I say, dismissing him in the only kind way I know how. Issac nods slowly and backs out of the front door.

"Bye, Kennedy," he says, throwing her an awkward smile that Kenni clearly appreciates. Finally, the redhead leaves the apartment, and the sound of the door shutting is my clue to freak out.

"This isn't yours?" I hiss, whirling on Drew so fast that she winces when she sees the intensity in my eyes.

"No. Brook, what the hell is going on?"

I start to pace like a madman in the living room. Kenni takes off the dishwashing gloves and comes to stand in the doorway, watching me walk back and forth.

"Did you guys lock the apartment when you left this morning?" I question.

"Yeah ...?" Kenni says.

"You're *sure no one else* was in here besides the three of us and Issac?" I demand.

"Brooklyn, you're scaring me. What's happening?" Drew demands. I stop walking around and stare at the beanie on the table.

"You know where that came from. You know who it belonged to," I whisper, taking measured breaths to calm myself down. "And you know she was wearing it the night she was abducted by a man in a mask saying he took her to get to me."

"Holy," Drew whispers, her mouth hanging open in disbelief. Then her eyes begin to well up with tears.

"You can't be serious, Brook," breathes Kenni, looking at the green fabric with horror.

"Someone got in here when we weren't in and put that on my desk just like they did with the USB," I reveal. Drew's eyes go wider.

"The *what*?" Kenni exclaims.

"A USB. The little memory stick thing that plugs into the computer," I say.

"And it had what on it, exactly?"

"A video of this guy in a creepy mask telling me that he'll take every last student to get me alone. He said I have to realize my actions have consequences."

There's dead silence in the apartment.

"Did you give it to Greenwood?" Drew finally pipes up, in a cracking voice.

"Yeah, I had to." Drew nods in approval.

"Good."

"How did he get in here?" Kenni whispers.

"I don't know. You guys didn't give anyone a key to our apartment, did you?" I ask.

"No."

"Nope."

"He must have picked the lock, then. It's old. It can't be that hard to pick," I reason, dropping on the couch and staring straight ahead. "I can't believe this is happening."

"You gonna give that to the police?" Kenni asks, nodding to the beanie. I shrug in quasi-defeat.

"I have to."

"Brook." I look at Drew. "Since when have you ever done anything that anyone actually *wanted* you to do?"

11

"Brooklyn!" I turn to the person saying my name and get punched across the face by an invisible fist. It knocks my teeth loose and offsets my jaw.

"Brook, help!" A girl says. This time I get kicked by a disembodied foot.

"BROOKLYN!" It's a shrieking man's voice. I'm stabbed in the gut with a knife when I try to run to help them. That happens over and over until I finally give up and collapse on the ground, letting the knife cut me repeatedly.

I yawn the next morning while sitting through my 10:00 a.m. class. Needless to say, I didn't get much sleep last night. When I gave the beanie to Greenwood this morning, I told him that I found it in my mailbox like the USB. There's no way I'm letting him know that someone's breaking into my apartment. Thankfully, Mask Man only seems to be concerned with my room, so my friends are safe. For now, anyway.

"Brooklyn!" I look at my professor. She has stopped her lecture to call me out in front of the entire 150-

person class. "You alright? Seems like you're somewhere else."

"Sorry, Professor. I'm fine," I say, giving a thin-lipped smile to the old woman.

"You want to tell us where you were?" she says, hiding her anger behind a fake smile. I flounder, my face flushed with red. Some students sitting behind me snicker. "I'm sure it was a beautiful place. But if you aren't here mentally, there's no point in being here." I open my mouth to retort but decide it's best not to say anything. My professor gives me a pathetic little shrug as though I'm a lost cause. "Maybe you'll be with us on Thursday. Until then," she says, gesturing to the door. With my head hung somewhat low and everyone's eyes on me, I pack my things and leave through the back door.

This professor always does that with the football players who sit in the back and fall asleep. She just tells them they're wasting their tuition sitting there napping and asks them to leave. In a way, I feel bad, but there's a guy who wants me dead, so I think I'm allowed to zone out.

I make my way to Rosenburg and sit down on a bench in a quiet hallway facing a window that looks over the road. Being alone isn't really my thing, especially when I'm being stalked again, but I just want to be by myself for a while. I close my eyes, enjoying the silence.

I wish I could see that video again. I want to hear his message over and over until it's burned into my mind. I want it memorized so I can recite it forwards and backwards. Last year with Taylor was different. I could research what the frat house did and why the underground brothers were possibly after me. I could gather DPS records and be conveniently friends with the descendant of the murdered and with the murderer.

But, this year, I'm alone.

It's a waiting game until Mask Man finally decides to show himself.

And when he does, I'll be ready with a baseball bat to smash his face in.

"Brooklyn?" says a familiar voice. I open my eyes and look to my left to see Jared Quinn, a freshman Delta Rho pledge and Nate's fraternity little brother. Even though he's a quiet kid, he's always kind and open with the people he knows. When I first met him, I had to pull information out of him just to carry on a conversation. Since then, though, whenever we see each other on campus, we always make sure to wave hello.

"Hey, Jared!" I exclaim, welcoming a new face.

"What are you doin' here?"

"I'm waiting for my next class," I lie. "How about you?"

"Same." He settles down next to me, and I scoot over. "How are you? Are you okay?"

"Yeah, I'm fine." Jared nods in approval and takes a shaky breath in. He clutches the shiny silver crucifix around his neck. I notice how his leg starts bouncing. "Question is, are *you* okay?" I ask with a little smile, seeing his knuckles turn pale holding the crucifix.

"No, I'm good! I just have a test next class."

"And God is gonna help you with that?" I ask. I feel bad the second my question comes out skeptically, but I can't take it back.

"I think He helps with everything. Even if it's the little stuff," Jared says. He notices how I'm trying to contain a scoff. "Not a big religion gal, huh?"

"I was never raised in a particular religion. I remember going to church a few times with my dad, and then we stopped going. We still celebrate Christmas, though," I say with a laugh. "What's God done for you?"

"Lots of stuff," says Jared, looking into the distance. "I prayed to him every night when my mom had melanoma, and she got better. Slowly, but she got better. And then when my grandpap on my dad's side lost his job and was going to lose his house, I prayed to God to help him. And wouldn't you know it, my grandpap got a second mortgage and didn't have to move." Jared smiles. "I know it's cliché, but He works in mysterious ways."

"And all you have to do to ask for help is ...?" I trail off. Jared looks at me like I'm kidding.

"Pray. Just put your hands together like this and ask Him for help." Jared demonstrates by putting his two palms together and lining up his fingers so they all point skyward. "He's got a lot of stuff to deal with, but He always has time for you. He listens." Jared seems to retreat into himself and looks at his lap, dropping his hands. "Sorry for the religion lesson."

"No worries at all," I say sincerely. "I could actually use some other-worldly help right now."

"Ask God. Seriously." Jared pauses, looking like he wants to ask another question. A reassuring look from me helps him along. "Help with what, if I can ask?"

"Just life stuff," I say, not wanting to worry him. "What have you been praying for recently?"

"Recently? The girl who disappeared." I turn to fully look at him, trying to keep a straight face. "It's terrible what happened to her. I pray that she gets home safely and that it doesn't happen again."

"That's sweet," I say genuinely. Jared puts his hand on my shoulder.

"Try it, Brooklyn. You seem to have a lot on your mind. I gotta run. Tell Nate I say hi if you see him."

"Likewise," I say as he gathers his things and leaves, waving goodbye sweetly. He's what Drew likes to call an "innocent freshman": a poor little kid blind to the reality and stress of college. I hope Jared can live in his bubble for as long as possible before it's broken by an internship or, worse, a serial killer.

My next class is in a building across from Rosenburg, and I zone out in that one too. I feel horrible for being distracted today, but I can't help it.

On the bus ride home, my phone rings, and I absentmindedly pick it up, not looking at the caller ID before pressing 'accept'. To my relief, it's Drew.

"Brook, when are you getting home?"

"I'm on the bus right now. Probably five minutes. What's up?"

"Greenwood just came by. He wants to talk to you." My stomach plummets. A CP officer going to your house to talk to you isn't a good sign. I knew this day would explode.

I trudge off the bus and make my way home. Sure enough, there's a CP car parked right outside of my apartment. Making sure to take measured breaths, I walk up to the car and see Greenwood inside flipping through a small notebook. I knock on the window. He gets out of the cruiser, puts his hands on his hips, and watches me through his tinted sunglasses.

"I wanted to talk to you," he says. I look around.

"Here? In a parking lot? Pretty Watergate, huh?" I say, trying not to sound like a wise ass.

"No. In your house." Another cop, with pitch black hair and a stony gaze, gets out of the car. He seems to be even younger than Greenwood. "This is my trainee, Officer Kenneth Lin. He's going to shadow me, especially when it concerns you."

"Awesome," I say sarcastically. "Well, follow me."

I open the door. Drew doesn't yell to greet me like she usually does. I think she wants to listen in behind her closed bedroom door rather than make her presence known. Frankly, I don't blame her. Greenwood and Lin sit at my table, and I sit across from them. Greenwood glances around my living room with a slightly disgusted look as though he was sitting in a dive bar.

"What's up?" I ask.

"We cracked the USB," says Greenwood, redirecting his eyes from the stained ceiling to me.

"And?" Lin takes a deep breath.

"There's no evidence to suggest that there was a video on it."

"*What?*" I say, looking incredulously from one officer to the other. "What about the beanie?"

"We ran some DNA tests on it, and it's clean. No prints, no hair, nothing. Must've been your roommate's," says Greenwood. I can almost hear Drew scoff from behind her door.

"You're joking," I say, perplexed.

"Wish I was." The young cop looks at me with the expression of someone who clearly hates the position he's in. "Now, unless you're lying or withholding information, which you can't do, it's a dead end."

100

"I'm not lying. Why would I lie about this?" I ask angrily.

"To stay in the spotlight. Prolong your fifteen minutes of fame," says Greenwood as if stating the obvious.

"I didn't even *want* the fame when it was around, Officer," I say through my teeth.

"What about withholding information?" Lin asks.

"I'm not doing that either. I get reprimanded if I do that," I remind the rookie. Lin looks like he's about to retort, but Greenwood jumps in.

"You watch how you speak to us, Perce," says Greenwood quickly. "We're going to open your mailbox and see what's in it."

"You could've opened it on your own. Why do you want me to do it?" I ask.

"So you can't hide anything." Greenwood leans in. "Unfortunately, as cops, we can't take people's word for granted."

I begrudgingly lead the pair outside and open my mailbox. Lin takes a flashlight out of his belt and shines it into the little, square metal box. Like I told them before, there's nothing in there, but, of course, they scour every inch of that tiny box and take a few samples before shutting and locking it. I don't want to say that I told them so, but I did. Lin looks to Greenwood.

"So, what do we do?" he asks his mentor.

"We take those samples to the lab and see what happens," Greenwood says. He looks to me. "And, as for you, keep giving us any evidence that you find. If this guy is real, he's going to communicate to the college at large through you. Keep an eye out on your end, and we'll do the same on ours."

"So, just to be clear, you don't believe me about the man?" I ask him as he starts to walk away. Greenwood does me the decency of turning around.

"I want to, Brooklyn. But, at this point, it's not looking promising," he says, eyeing me with pity, like I'm such a fragile person.

"Why wouldn't you believe me? I was right last year."

"A lot has happened since last year, especially in regard to you." Greenwood nods. "Just concentrate on schoolwork and try to adjust to normal life."

The cops leave me standing on the curb. I watch as they walk away, my eyes burning holes in their backs.

^^^

For the rest of the night, I do as Greenwood asks and concentrate on the readings and lessons that I missed in class today. As I go over the slideshow online, I realize I didn't miss much, and my professor was being overly dramatic.

A yawn comes over me again. I'm tired all the time, which explains my irritability and temper. I won't get anywhere with Nicole's disappearance, my friends, or my classwork if every single little thing sets me off. After closing my eyes for a few minutes and concentrating on my breathing, I feel slightly calmer. If I manage to finish my homework early, maybe I can go to bed earlier tonight and catch up on sleep.

Around six, I make my way to the kitchen and quickly peek through the living room window. The sky is pitch black. Air pollution, courtesy of the city of Northwich, blocks the stars from view. I let the curtain drop and go back to the kitchen to boil a pot of water for pasta. Drew is still holed up in her room, and I can only assume it's going to be a long night for Kenni at the library. I've been to the library but Kenni spends so much time there that she should just pitch a tent and unroll a sleeping bag.

It's then that Nate and Kienan burst into my apartment.

I jump about a foot in the air, cursing myself under my breath for not having locked the door. The door slams shut recklessly behind them. Nate comes into the kitchen as Kienan turns the corner and walks past the bathroom to open Kennedy's door.

"Not in here!" says Kienan.

"Um, hello to you too!" I call down the hallway to him. I look at Nate, absolutely baffled by their sudden appearance. "What's going on?" I ask as Nate breathes like he just ran a 5k.

"Issac didn't come home tonight," he says.

"Did you call him?"

"Didn't pick up. Tried texting too."

"When was his last class?"

"Supposed to end four hours ago."

"And he just never came home?"

"If he came home, Kienan wouldn't be tearing through Kenni's room," Nate points out. Right on cue, I hear something in Kennedy's room hit the ground.

"Sorry!" yells Kienan.

"How do you know his phone isn't dead?"

"Because he carries a charger on him always."

"Let's not sound the alarm yet," I warn, despite the black hole that's forming in my stomach. So much for the meditation earlier.

"Brook, they said Nicole was missing after she didn't come home."

"Yeah, and if I sent out a missing person request every time Kenni didn't come home from the library, the cops would hate me more than they already do. He's probably in a dining hall or something and can't find an outlet," I reason, trying to calm my boyfriend down. Nate looks like he might throw up. He starts to pace up and down the hallway.

"Brook, c'mon, at a time like this, Issac not coming home is a bit *too* coincidental," argues Nate. "They sounded the alarm pretty damn quick on Nicole." I can't argue with that. At the sound of Nate's feet falling heavy on the floor, Drew pokes her head out of her room.

"Uh-oh, Pretty Boy's in distress again," quips Drew.

"You're goddamn right I am, Drew. Issac didn't come home tonight," Nate says.

"He's probably hanging out with a friend on main campus or something. It's only six," Drew says reasonably.

"Thank you!" I say, taking a box of pasta out of the cabinet. "While you're here, you want pasta?"

"Sure," says Kienan as he comes back from Kennedy's room, clearly not as rigid as my boyfriend.

"Not that hungry," bites Nate, going into the living room to sit on the edge of the couch. I dump pasta into the boiling pot, then go to stand in front of him.

"Nate, hon, calm down, please. You're gonna give yourself a heart attack," I say with a little smile.

"Brook—"

"*Nate.*" I squat down so I'm looking up at his face. "Take a deep breath in and out for me. It'll be okay."

"Did your buddy, Gavin, tell you that? That it'll all be okay?" Nate looks into my eyes without flinching. Now, it's my turn to be dramatic.

"*What?*" I say. "What does *he* have to do with *anything?"* Nate shakes his leg out of nerves.

"I saw the way you were looking at him in Rosenburg the other day."

"You must be kidding me," I say in disbelief, backing away from him. "You burst into my apartment looking for Issac and now you're accusing me of *flirting* with a *freshman.* How is that relevant *at all?* You're just trying to pick a fight because you're angry about Issac."

"Yeah, I am. I am angry." Nate's lips have become a thin line, and his nostrils are flared. "That kid was into you. You're observant. You must've seen it." He's becoming tenser by the second, and I'm not the person he wants to fight with right now. I force myself to breathe slowly, but it does nothing to help me.

"Okay, well, Gavin is a *freshman.* I've met him *twice.* If he's into me, that's his problem. I'm with you. I wouldn't be if I didn't love you." For the first time ever, Nate looks at me, with hateful eyes. He doesn't believe me. A lump is forming in my throat, but I refuse to cry. "Why is this coming out now, huh? Why don't you believe me?"

"You didn't tell him to stop!"

"Yeah, and you didn't tell Jordyn to either!" As soon as I say it, I want to take it back. I shouldn't be escalating things, but the anger that's been building up in me is now bursting out. The apartment is silent. Kienan and Drew don't dare say anything. Nate stands up, fury in his eyes.

"Don't you bring her into this," he says through his teeth.

"Oh, I'm *absolutely* bringing her into this. You think *Gavin* was flirting with me? If you think *that* was bad, you're oblivious to when she's around you, Nate," I exclaim.

"Okay, now you're just picking a fight," Nate waves away. I laugh out loud at his absurdity.

"Holy shit, are you *kidding me*?! I thought it was grievance-airing hour, so I'm just continuing what you started!"

"I don't even *like* her, Brook. She's Kienan's friend!"

"How is that *any* different from Gavin?" I lash. Nate seems stumped by that one, but he keeps going anyway.

"Oh, come *on*, Brooklyn—"

"No, *you* come on, Nate! It's the *exact same thing*. Your double standard bullshit is fucking *infuriating*!" My voice catches in my throat. Drew has her hands over her mouth, frozen where she stands. Kienan is just gaping at us. Nate's eyes now look sorry, but his face is petrified with shock. I take a deep breath and compose myself. As my anger dissipates into the air, I begin to realize the true meaning of what I've just said. Everything seems heavy, even the air I laboriously drag into my lungs. No one wants to say a word.

It's then that the pot of water on the stove boils over and sends hot water onto the stovetop.

12

Now I've gone and done it. The one solid good thing I had in my life is gone. Though, with me being tense all the time, it was bound to happen at some point. Sure, Nate was out of line bringing up Gavin, but I'd escalated things, allowing all my negative feelings to burst out of me in a destructive tornado of hate. Some of it was aimed at him, but most of it came from personal worries and frustrations. Regardless, I know I have to set things right.

Later that night, I knock on Nate's apartment door. Half of me wonders if he'll just leave me out here to freeze in the cold air. The other half still has faith in him but also wants to slap some sense into him.

Kienan opens the door. He smiles so tightly that his lips make one thin line, says nothing, and lets me in. I don't find Jordyn lounging on the couch or sitting at the table, which is a good sign. I swallow my pride and gently nudge the door to Nate's room open.

My boyfriend is lying on his mattress. He's got one hand behind his head as he stares at the ceiling. He doesn't look my way when I come in. I quietly shut the door behind me and lean against the back of it.

"Nate," I say in a low voice. He doesn't seem to hear me, and I'm not sure if I want to press my luck. "Hey." He finally sits up and looks at me. My breath hitches for a moment when I see his face. *That's* why he didn't automatically sit up. He didn't want me to see his tired, red eyes. He's been crying. Nate chews on his bottom lip and looks at me, wondering if it's a good idea to stand and approach me. I hold out my hand to let him know that it's okay. Nate gets up and takes my hand, looking into my eyes with all the regret in the world.

"Brook, I'm ..." Wordlessly, I bring him into a hug. He gladly puts his arms around me and buries his face in my hair. I put mine on his chest and just breathe. We stand there like that forever. My arms start to hurt, but even then, I don't let go.

"I'm so sorry, Brooklyn," he breathes, his voice shaky like he's going to cry again. "I'm ... I'm just *so scared.*"

"Me too," I reassure him. I pull away from him and look up into his red puffy face. My thumb gently wipes away the little droplets of water on his cheeks. He smiles like he's embarrassed and gazes down at me.

"I'm sorry for going off on you like that. I love you so much. No one could ever change that," he whispers.

"I'm sorry for yelling back. I know I've been a handful, but I'm so thankful to have you around. I love you too." I squeeze him one last time, then let him go. The clock on his desk says it's 11 o'clock. "Did Issac come home?" Nate shakes his head.

"No. Kienan is texting Issac's engineering friends and the frat guys to see if they've heard from him. Nothing so far." Nate opens the door for me, and we sit down on the couch, underneath the Delta Rho flag. Our shoulders touch as we look at the black TV, hypnotized by the blank screen. "What if he's gone, Brook?"

"I don't want to think about it," I murmur. Nate gulps and stares at the floor.

"Have they found anything else on Nicole yet?"

"I found a green beanie on my desk, the one Nicole was wearing the night she was kidnapped. I gave it to the cops, but there's nothing on it. No fingerprints, no hair, nothing. Greenwood said it was probably Drew's. And then he said there's no evidence a video was ever on that USB. He thinks I'm lying," I recount.

"He's a prick," Nate says.

"Tell me about it. He had this other trainee cop, Kenneth Lin. That poor man," I say. Nate snorts.

"Poor guy," Nate echoes. "So, what do we do if Issac doesn't come home by midnight?"

"We call the cops and say he never came home. And they take it from there," I say.

"And you tell Greenwood?"

"Have to."

"That's really the *worst* thing from last year. You sent a kid to jail, and the other ones are either under house arrest or suspended from school, but the cops keeping tabs on you is the worst. Can't even drink without one of 'em breathing down your neck," Nate says.

"Yeah, no kidding."

"Guys!" Kienan exclaims, running into the room somewhat out of breath. "One of his friends, Fletcher, said he got on the bus with Issac three hours ago and thought he was going home." Nate jumps up.

"Okay, he was coming home. So, what happened to him?"

"Let's go to the bus stop and see if there's anything there. No stone unturned, right?" I suggest. Kienan nods and goes to his room to get his coat. Nate tosses me his jacket from the closet behind the front door. Once we're set to brave the cold, we exit the apartment.

I can see my breath in the air as I walk with a boy on either side of me to the bus stop. We all walk purposefully, our feet making solid contact with the ground and our steps echoing. There's no one in the little bus shelter when we approach. Kienan takes a look around as Nate turns on his phone's flashlight and whacks through the frozen grass with his foot. The wind whistles a bit, making the cold worse. I brace myself against a particularly large gust that stirs up the leaves on the road and makes them blow in an ominous circle.

"There's nothing here," Nate determines.

"The bus didn't get hijacked or anything. We would've heard about it," I reason.

"Could've gotten off at the wrong stop," muses Kienan.

"He's an engineering major, and we've been here for almost four months. Kid's smarter than that," Nate says. Frustrated, I walk in a circle, looking this way and that, trying to figure out what could've happened to Nate's roommate. He got on the bus and never got off. Something must've happened to him when he—

Snap.

The boys look towards me as I step on something that sounds like plastic. I look down and raise my boot. There, on the wet pavement, is Issac's RUID card. I carefully pick it up, brush off the melting snow, and examine it under the streetlamp light. It hasn't been defaced in any way, just cast aside while someone was probably wrestling Issac to the ground.

"Brook, turn it over," says Nate in a shaky voice. I do what he says and swallow hard. In black marker, it reads, "*ANOTHER ONE DOWN.*"

"Shit," I whisper.

"Are there any tracks in the snow?" Kienan asks, looking at the ground. Unfortunately, the salt they've put on the road has melted away the flakes. There's no sign of a scuffle. Suddenly, Kienan perks up.

"Did you guys hear that?" he says, quickly turning around.

"Hear what?" Nate snorts.

"That scream." We all fall silent, our ears straining to hear sounds besides passing cars. I pick up some birds chirping, the revving of a motorcycle waiting at the stoplight outside of the housing complex, and a dog barking. No screaming to be heard.

"Dude, come on. You're screwing with us," Nate waves away. Though I don't say anything, I agree with Nate.

"No, no! Listen again. I swear I heard something," Kienan insists. We continue to stand there, hugging ourselves from the cold. My toes begin to go numb, so I bounce on the balls of my feet. I'm about to turn around and call it a night, until I hear an extremely faint scream in the distance.

"I heard *that*," I mutter, ceasing my bouncing. I grip Issac's ID in my hand and start to walk towards the entrance to West Campus. Nate and Kienan jog a bit to catch up with me, but I keep going. My feet carry me across the busy intersection and stop when they hit the sidewalk diagonally from where they started.

"There's no way," says Nate, slightly out of breath from having to dodge cars to keep up. "He can't be in there."

What we're looking at is one of the many corners of the 150-acre Sunset Cemetery. The tombstones cast long and ghoulish shadows in the lights of passing cars. Venturing deeper means encountering older crumbling chapels, tombs, and gang members who enter the cemetery at night and prey on the kids who happen to wander in, stoned or drunk. During the day, Sunset is a beautiful place to walk, run, and explore. I remember Drew used to sit there on a blanket and study for finals on nice spring days, but none of us would ever enter the cemetery at night. Not unless we wanted to risk getting shot.

"Oh, fuck no, I'm not going in there," Kienan backs out, his voice trembling. I stare into the black depths of the place, thinking of Issac being dragged through the broken decrepit tombstones. I must look intent because Nate grabs my forearm.

"*We* aren't gonna go in there. We're gonna call the police." Nate turns to me. "Right, Brook?" I bite my tongue and smile.

"Right." I pull my arm out of Nate's grasp and sharply spin around to walk back across the intersection, making cars stop for me.

^^^

I hand over Issac's ID to Greenwood and his trainee the next day. He looks angry that I've given him more work, but he begrudgingly takes it and turns it over in his hand.

"Thanks for this. Poor kid's probably out there right now," says Lin, a pitiful look on his face.

"Yeah, well, the FBI'll find him I'm sure." The ID is tossed onto Greenwood's desk carelessly. Once I push past his tone, my ears perk up.

"The *FBI*?" I reiterate. Greenwood nods.

"Yes. The school is kicking around bringing them on campus. Personally, I think the city police department and our crew are doing just fine, but—"

"They handle things like this?" I say.

"If they suspect something like domestic terrorism is involved. In this case, it might be a hostage situation. Or it might just be a routine kidnapper out for a joy ride." Greenwood sits back behind his desk. "Either way, they'll figure it out."

"I think it might be both. The guy might be trying to make a name for himself," Lin ponders.

"In Northwich, New York?" I ask.

"It's a mid-sized city, just large enough for someone to blend in with a crowd. The city isn't comparable with Boston or New York City, but he might be starting out here to see if he can hack it in a larger place," explains Lin. I'm thankful that he doesn't speak to me with Greenwood's patronizing snark.

"How do you know it's a guy?"

"You ask too many questions for your own good," Greenwood tells me, clearly wanting me to leave his office.

"I'm at college. It's my job to ask questions, Officer." The last three syllables are hard to push out of my mouth. Greenwood sneers at me, but Lin chimes in.

"A higher percentage of kidnappers are male, and they usually go after younger girls. This is interesting, considering the person we have seems to be interested in taking older kids. Quite irregular, but still enough to cause an alarm," replies Lin. I give him a grateful smile.

"Whole situation is weird," Greenwood surmises. He stares at me and puts his hands out like he's confused. "Why are you still here? Don't you have class or something?"

"I appreciate your concern," I say. Greenwood smirks as I leave his office.

Whenever I sit, my leg bounces on the floor nervously. I know what I have to do after class. No part of me wants to do it, but I have nowhere else to turn. I need information that only a certain person can give me. Nate texts me, asking if I want to grab dinner at the student center later, but I tell him I'm studying. When Finn comes over to say hello to Drew and invites me to watch a movie with them, I say I'll have to pass. I have other plans tonight that surprisingly don't involve going into the cemetery.

The Uber picks me up around 6:00. I get into the car, say hello to my driver, and then stay silent for the rest of the ride. My destination is about twenty minutes north of here, in a quiet little suburbia outside of Northwich. The houses all look the same, no doubt all developed in the 60's by the same person, who gave them the same siding, windows, and doors. The driver pulls up to a small two-story house that has seen better days and parks the car, looking around.

"This is it," he says. "Have a good one."

"You too." I take my backpack and sling it over my shoulder. Once I slam the car door shut, the Uber screeches away, and I'm left alone on an unlit street. I swallow hard and walk up the concrete front steps to the porch, where a rocking chair is rotting outside of the largest window. There are pots full of dirt that I can only assume housed plants at one point. A smaller container has a dying rose plant in it. Someone was trying to make it climb up and over the front door, but it couldn't make the journey. I quickly rap three times on the white door and stand back, hoping to God that someone will answer. Or better yet, if they don't, I can leave and pretend I was never here. But I need answers. The person who lives here might know something I don't, which is why I want someone to open the door.

And someone does.

Ryker Williams stands there in grey sweatpants, a loose t-shirt with a V-neck, and athletic white socks. There's more stubble than I'm used to seeing on his chin, and his green eyes aren't vibrant anymore. They widen when they see me. He suddenly looks awake as he stares at me with a gleeful horror, an expression that starts a little whirlpool in the pit of my stomach.

"Hey, Ryker. Can I come in?" I ask, a hopeful little smile on my face. Ryker stays silent, his mouth agape, but opens the door anyway. I carefully step inside.

It's a small space, but for a kid living with just his mother, it's large enough. The walk through the front door leads us into the living room, which is stuffed with two couches on opposite walls, a coffee table in between, a standard lamp in the corner, and a small TV on the mantle of the fireplace on the far wall. A doorway to the left of the TV leads to a dining room, and the adjoining room, I assume, is the kitchen. Ryker just stares at me in awe as I stand in the living room, trying not to look as uncomfortable as I feel.

"Why are you here?" he finally says. I hike my backpack up further on my shoulder and nod.

"I need to talk with you. Alone." Almost as if on cue, a woman enters the room. She's in her mid to late fifties and has green eyes like her son's and brown hair with grey strands that are poking through like weeds. I recognize her immediately as Ms. Williams, the woman who broke down crying in court when her son was sentenced to six months of house arrest, followed by another six months of community service. Her face becomes hard when she sees me. Ryker looks like he wants her to disappear.

"What are *you* doing in my house?" She says like she's talking to a cockroach crawling on the wall.

"I invited her here, Mom," Ryker lies, turning to his mother and giving her a pointed look.

"You should've asked me, Ryker. I wouldn't've let this piece of trash into my home," she spits.

"Mom—" Ryker tries to stop her, but she takes a few steps towards me. I stand my ground despite my fright. Her livid expression indicates she thinks she can make me disappear if she stares at me long enough.

"You send my son to court, get him sentenced to house arrest, get him expelled from college, and you have the goddamn *nerve* to show up in my house?" Ms. Williams grits her teeth and shakes her head. "It's *your* fault he's like this, you know."

"Well, maybe if your son wasn't an accessory to attempted murder, we wouldn't be in this position," I say in a deadpan, already over her spiteful attitude. I can tell she's debating slapping me. Thankfully, Ryker steps in before anything serious happens.

"Let's go to my room," he says, putting a hand on my shoulder and glancing at his mother. "C'mon, Brooklyn." Ryker gently leads me away from his mother whose eyes follow me as we go up the stairs to his room.

The bedroom I'm taken into is clean, like I expected it to be. The bed is nicely made, the knick-knacks on the desk are organized, and the dresser drawers are all perfectly shut with no clothes peeking out of the tops. Ryker shuts the door and sits down in his desk chair. I figure I'm allowed to sit down too, so I sit on his bed, placing my backpack on the floor. Ryker's eyes watch me the entire time. When I'm settled, he shrugs indignantly.

"So, why are you here?" he asks again.

"I needed to talk to you. Trust me, I'm not here because I want to be."

"You could've texted. Or called."

"You were never on your phone."

"I'm on it all the time these days," says Ryker, with an unamused expression. "Now that I have nothing to do."

"Be glad you're not in prison. You're at home, you can sleep in a bed, and you have homemade food," I say.

"It's the same after a while. I can't leave," says Ryker tartly. "Sometimes, I think it might be easier if I were in jail."

"Don't say that," I respond, throwing him a reproachful look. "We both know that's not true."

"What? Me saying it or me thinking it? Because I've done both." Ryker rests his elbows on his knees and peers at me with narrowed eyes. "But, luckily for you, I'm not in prison, so you can just show up at my house, make my mom angry, and surprise the hell out of me."

"You're pissed at me, too?"

117

"Yeah, I am. You said you hoped I rot in jail, and now that I'm not doing that, I've got this thing." That's when Ryker reaches down and pulls up the left leg of his pants to reveal a metal bracelet clamped around his ankle. I knew he had one of those, but it's a bit jarring to see it. The metal thing has a little blinking light, which I think means Ryker is being monitored. "Fuckin' thing itches and taking showers? Forget about it." He lets go of it and looks back up at me, with a little gleam in his eyes. "But I'm proud of you. Because I deserve this. All of us deserved what was coming to us. And getting justice from you was just the icing on the cake." He sounds like he's actually admiring me for holding him captive in his own house. "And if you show up at my house, unannounced, without your little CP gang in tow, there's gotta be a good reason why." My body uncomfortably adjusts itself on top of his comforter.

"Have you been keeping up with the news?"

"I try to, yeah."

"So, you know about the disappearances of Nicole Walters and Issac Reed?"

"Yeah, I heard ..." He raises an eyebrow. "These wouldn't have anything to do with *you,* now, would they?" I bite the inside of my cheek, and my silence answers his question. "Jesus Christ, *still?*"

"You don't know of anyone on campus who would—?"

"No. They sniffed all of us out. How do you know for sure this is connected to SHA, though? Is it just an assumption?"

"No, I received a USB from an unknown man in a mask, who spoke in an altered deep voice, who basically said that I had to realize there were consequences to my actions, and I have to pay for what I've done." I'm getting tired of repeating that. Seeing everyone's reaction, though, is interesting. Ryker simply falls silent. He just stares at me with his mouth slightly open.

"Holy shit," he finally groans, running a hand through his scruffy self-cut hair. "You're serious?"

"Unfortunately."

"You told the cops?"

"I have to tell them everything. It's part of this agreement I have with them after last year. It's basically punishment for not going to them in the first place and figuring out the mystery on my own, which I think I did a good job of doing." I stop myself from ranting. I've talked too much about CP in the past six months. "But, yeah. I've told them everything. And apparently, they're thinking of bringing in the FBI." I look at him as he thinks through what I've just told him. "You wouldn't know of *anyone* who would still be out for me?"

"The guy who wanted you dead the most is in jail, Brooklyn. I don't know anyone out there who would want to come after you." He pauses. "You should go to prison and ask him. He'd sure *love* to see you."

"I wouldn't do that even if I was desperate," I scoff, crossing my legs and arms. "You think I want to see his face ever again?"

"I wouldn't if I were you," Ryker sympathizes. "But to answer your question, I don't know of anyone on campus who would want to get you. The cops weeded out everyone in the frat, and they're all gone as far as I'm concerned. There's no *student* who has it out for you."

"Alright." There's a silence as Ryker looks at me with pity.

"I can't believe this is happening again," he quietly mutters.

"You and me both," I agree. "Why do they always come after me?"

"You can't help it. You're just so stalkable," Ryker jokes. The scoff that makes its way out of me is cut short by me biting my lip. "You laugh, but it's true. There's something about you that just begs for someone to hunt you."

"It's exhausting. I have nightmares about it all the time."

Ryker looks guilty, breaking eye contact with me for a moment to look at the floor. He's the reason for most of the terrors I experience, but I don't tell him that. I stand up and put my backpack over my left shoulder. Ryker gets up too and puts his hands in his pockets. He walks over to the bed and stands in front of me, so I raise my eyes to see his face. He has a look in his eyes that I can't quite place, but it throws me off a bit. I try to pass him by, but there's no way I can leave unless he steps back.

"I should probably go. I think your mom is getting ready to kill me downstairs." Ryker gently takes my hands from my sides and holds my fingers in his. I look down and then look back up at him. The poor thing looks so lonely and dejected that it's hard not to feel bad for the once-great student manager of WRDW. Ryker snorts softly and examines my face.

"I missed you a lot, Brooklyn," he admits in a deeper voice.

"You still kidnapped me, Ryker. Nothing you say is going to make me forget that," I say, taking my fingers out of his grasp.

"I know, but that's what I love about you. You still hate me after last year." I open my mouth to say something, but I can't find the words. "Your persistence is crazy, Brooklyn. That's part of what makes you so goddamn attractive."

"Ryker," I warn.

"What?" Ryker whispers. His eyes are lidded. "What, Brooklyn?" I try to find words, but it's hard to do it when I realize how close he is to me.

"You were pissed at me two minutes ago," I finally breathe in disbelief.

"Then I remembered: you're Brooklyn. I could never stay mad at you. Even if you did trap me here."

I scoff slightly at his response. Ryker takes a step forward so his body is inches away from mine. For a second, I get caught up in it, letting my eyes drift shut even though I'm in the presence of the guy who trapped me in his car. Then I realize how crazy I'm being.

"What are you doing?" I say tightly. I partially say it to myself since I hear the voice of my conscience screaming at me to pull away, but, for some reason, I'm rooted to the floor. I push him away, looking at him with timid eyes.

"Just ... thinking," he trails off. Ryker backs up a few inches.

"About?" I ask.

"What if ... you kept me in the loop with this investigation? I could help you," he offers.

"Yeah?"

"Yeah. I have nothing better to do anyway." I don't have anything to say for once. Ryker steps closer and hooks his thumbs in the belt loops of my jeans, pulling me towards him. My intestines feel like a dog is chewing on them. "I know a lot of shit. I was their leader. I can

121

tell you everything." Ryker puts his forehead on mine, and I instinctively put my hands on his shoulders, firmly pushing him backward, but he doesn't move. He seems to want to kiss me, badly. His lips are parted, I hear his breath quicken, and his eyes are lidded. His mouth is mere millimeters from mine. A sick feeling overcomes me. "Let me help you, Brooklyn."

"Get away from me, and I will," I test. Ryker swallows, pauses for a moment, then reluctantly does what I ask. My heart is pounding in my ears at the thought of what we've almost done. He looks at me like he's admiring every line and scar on my face. "I'm with Nate."

"Still?" he says, clearly let down. I nod. Ryker smiles in spite of himself. "Right. Who wouldn't love a frat guy?"

"Ryker," I warn as I lift my pack up higher on my shoulder.

"You should break up with him," Ryker says, stepping towards me with a flirtatious grin. I bite the inside of my cheek as he looks at me with a smile.

"And *you* should keep your opinions to yourself," I say pointedly.

"I don't know why you'd listen to anything I'd say. You were never one for listening," Ryker reasons. I let out a short laugh and back up to the door. Ryker's eyes are on me the entire way. "I'll walk you out."

He leads me downstairs as I replay the moment in his room over and over in my mind. I suspect I'm going to do that repeatedly throughout the night. His offer is tempting for sure, but it comes with a catch: Him. Ryker clearly hasn't gotten over whatever he felt toward me last year, and I assume my visit tonight only rekindled his feelings. When we get to the front door, I turn and nod to him. I make sure to keep my distance so he doesn't try to kiss me goodnight.

"If I figure out anything, I'll let you know," I say affirmatively.

"Good girl." He takes my hand and squeezes it. "Night, Brooklyn." He nods at me, drops my hand, and, like nothing ever happened, opens the door. When I walk out and it shuts behind me, I lean on the side of his house and let out a breath of relief, letting my heart calm down.

13

Thursday morning, I walk into WRDW and try to parse out the weekend stories that need to run. I assign each story to a reporter, send them an email, and ask if they feel comfortable covering a story independently over the weekend. Usually, I give larger projects like these to the seniors and juniors who need them for their portfolios as they apply for jobs and internships, but, every once in a while, I give a weekend story to a freshman. Needless to say, my little protégé isn't getting one, at least not until he learns to respect me.

News of Issac's disappearance has made its way around campus. A few of the fraternities and sororities are holding impromptu events on self-defense techniques, this weekend. It's not the disappearance that has everyone on edge, but the fact that this is the second one and the person behind them hasn't been caught. No one has a clue regarding their identity or what they could possibly want.

No one, that is, except me. And CP. And, if we're lucky, the FBI.

I sit through my classes. Thankfully, my professor in my last class doesn't kick me out again. When she dismisses us, I make the walk to the counseling center for my weekly session. My nightmares have only gotten worse, but there's no way I can tell Margaret. She needs to feel like she's making progress and not like I'm regressing. When the receptionist calls my name, I follow Margaret into her office where she shuts the door and we assume the position of therapist and patient.

"How are you?" I ask her in an artificial tone.

"The better question is, how are *you*?" she responds. "I know these disappearances have rattled everyone."

"Yeah, it's pretty scary," I agree, looking out of the window as always. There are even fewer leaves on the trees now. Most of the ones hanging on are either burnt brown or deep red. They look like they're just barely attached to their branches, waiting for the right gust of wind to blow them away.

"Were you close with them? The students who were taken?"

"Yeah. I knew both of them actually." Margaret scribbles something down on her pad.

"If I may ask, how?"

"Nicole was one of Drew's best friends. Issac was Nate's roommate, and my other roommate, Kennedy, had a crush on him." Margaret keeps scribbling. I try to look over at the pad, but I can't read her handwriting even if it's the right side up, let alone upside down. "If you don't mind my asking, what do you write down?" She looks up from the paper and gives me a reassuring smile.

"What we talk about in our sessions, concerns you may have, things of that nature. That way, I can look back to determine if there are any patterns or irregularities in your behavior," she explains.

"What was I talking about at this time last year?" I request.

Margaret goes into her drawer full of files, thumbs through them, and pulls out a red one with my name on it. In the file are a few loose papers and legal pad upon legal pad of her nonsensical scribbles. The small folder is bursting with notepads. She finds the one she's looking for, pulls it out, and flips through a few pages.

"Well, campus was still reeling from the uncovering of the fraternity. You said you were tired of people pestering you about how you solved the case, and you were sick of recounting the entire story to officials." I look back out of the window.

"Wow. Little did I know how sick of it I would be in a year," I mutter to myself. Margaret puts the file away and matter-of-factly picks up the notepad she's working on.

"Oh, you said last time you were going to see your father. How did that go?" asks Margaret, in a chipper voice.

"I still don't like him. Nothing he'll ever say or do or buy for me will change that," I tell her. "My mom says he's just concerned for my well-being, which would be believable, but he's never cared before. He never calls, texts, hell, *emails*. And I know this isn't what it's supposed to be, our relationship. My friends have open conversations with their fathers, and they're loved and cared for. I don't think I've ever had that." My shoulders slump involuntarily. "I'll just never make him proud, no matter what."

"I'm sure your father is proud of you," says Margaret, creasing her eyebrows in confusion. I shake my head and look at her.

"No, you don't understand. He tells me he's proud, but he still acts the same way. He pops into my life whenever it's convenient for him, and he's gone just as fast. He's never going to be consistently there for me, and I've come to accept that." Margaret looks like she's going to cry, and I feel as though I should take back my words, but the damage is done. "Are you alright?"

"Yes, yes, I'm fine," Margaret says, waving me off and sniffling a bit. I feel like handing her the tissues that sit on her desk, like she's always done for me. "Anything else happen between now and our last session?"

"Actually, yeah," I say, suddenly remembering what happened the other day at Ryker's. "This is all confidential, right?"

"Yes, of course," says Margaret, suddenly happy that I'm deciding to open up on my own for once. "What's going on?"

"Well, I wanted to ... follow up on the case," I start slowly, choosing my words carefully. "And I saw one of the boys who kidnapped me last year. Ryker, my boss at the station. And after we talked, we got *really* close together. Like, *very very* close." When I say that, Margaret bristles as I stare at the carpet just beyond the back of her chair. "I asked him to back up, and he did, but it was so odd."

"Did you have any physical contact with him beyond that?" Margaret asks, trying to mask the tightness in her voice.

"No, no. And Nate doesn't know, but I'm afraid he's going to find out I even went to see him," I tell her.

"Why do you have any reason to be afraid? You two have a good relationship from what I gather, very supportive and respectful."

"We do, we do. It's just I feel as though we've been on rocky footing lately. Last year's events didn't help much either, trust issues and all that. Nate has never liked Ryker, and I think he's always known Ryker had feelings for me. I don't voluntarily talk about him in front of Nate, I don't bring up the kidnapping, nothing like that, because I know he'll get angry." I bite my lip. Before I can even think twice about saying them, the words come out. "I feel like a bad person for visiting Ryker without telling Nate."

"Oh, Brooklyn. You're not a bad person," reassures Margaret, smiling sympathetically. "Your boyfriend doesn't dictate where you go or who you can or can't see. You're your own boss. If you thought visiting Ryker was the right thing to do, then it was. Nate can't take that away from you." Even though what she's saying make sense, it doesn't stop the swirling sensation in my stomach. I stare at the leaves out of the window again. There's one left hanging onto its branch for dear life.

^^^

When I get on the bus to go home, I just sink into the hard, cold plastic chair and close my eyes. It's been a long day of news stories and dodging the CP and city police officers that have overrun the campus. Thankfully, there are no FBI vans to be seen. I'm trying to understand why they think a bunch of uniformed men standing around will deter anyone from doing anything nefarious, but I'm not the chief of police however much I wish I were.

When I get home, I'm alone in my apartment. I automatically lock the door behind me and wait a second before walking further into my house. My room is freezing, so I turn up the heat and sit at my desk. I'm about to put my head down and rest my eyes for a few moments, but on my desk is a pair of black thick-rimmed plastic glasses. The lenses in them are cracked but are still holding together. I recognize them as the frames that were worn by a certain Delta Rho redhead.

"Dammit," I say to myself as I gingerly pick them up by an arm. I want to know how Mask Man can get in and out of my locked apartment, without taking or touching anything else. He doesn't seem to go into Kenni or Drew's room either, just mine.

I look at the wall in front of my desk and stare at the white stucco, trying to drill holes in it with my gaze. I know what I have to do, but I don't want to do it alone. But alone is the only way I might get face-to-face with Mask Man. My feet pick me up and carry me to my closet, where I put on a leather jacket with a hood that I borrowed from Drew and never gave back. It's big on her, but I can see why she wears it so often: it's very warm, warmer than other jackets I have. I stuff my RUID and key into one pocket and my phone in the other, and, after taking one last look at Issac's glasses, I leave.

The temperature outside has dropped by several degrees since I arrived home ten minutes ago. As I note the setting sun, I decide it's best to work quickly to avoid getting stuck out here alone. I walk to the edge of the

West Campus complex and then cross the road twice to get to the sidewalk bordering the graveyard. After I flip the hood up on the leather jacket as an act of attempted confidence, I begin to walk into the creepy grassy hellhole.

The farther into the graveyard I go, the more I'm reminded of cliché scenes in horror movies, where lone girls are slaughtered by what appear to be mere shadows. The further back I travel, the more broken and decayed everything is, the trees, the headstones, the tombs. I check over my shoulder every so often to make sure I'm not being followed. Typically, I always feel like there's someone behind me, but that sense is heightened tenfold as I keep moving forward.

Humming to myself to try to distract from the uneasy feeling in my stomach doesn't mitigate the terror I feel. I want to turn tail and run, but that wouldn't help anyone. Hell, I'm not even sure Issac is here. He could be anywhere, but I'm just aimlessly walking through this 150-acre graveyard, hoping to stumble on some clue.

Snap.

I turn around as my eyes dart every direction, hoping to see someone. When I look down, I realize that I've stepped on a twig. After grumbling at my own stupidity, I keep trekking on.

Eventually, I arrive at the very back of the graveyard near the train tracks and the highway, where I see two little chapels a short distance from each other. The one closest to me looks newer but well-used. The stone steps are a bit worn out at the front of the little gothic building, but other than that, it seems like it's been standing for a while. The one down the gravel road, though, is a wreck. Graffiti covers every inch of it, the windows are boarded up, the front steps are knocked out, and the paneling that's supposed to protect the bell tower from the harsh Northwich winter is on the ground, at the foot of the dirty red door. Somewhere inside me, I know this is where Issac and Nicole are being held, but how would Kienan hear a scream all the way from the road, which is about two miles in the opposite direction? Maybe we were making things up after all.

I look around to make sure no one is near, then walk around to the back of the church, fighting back dead pricker bushes and overgrown branches with my tall black boots. With one last glance over my shoulder, I kick at a brittle wooden panel covering a window. It shatters on impact, the plywood sending shards everywhere. I brush away the splintered wood and step into the abandoned chapel.

I've stepped onto the high alter, looking down at the cracked, broken, and decrepit pews. Graffiti in bright and faded colors blankets every inch of the inside of this place. The once beautiful stained-glass windows are in pieces all over the floor. There's little to no light, but what little light there is shows all of the dust and particles floating around in the air. A destroyed crucifix lies at my feet, and the steps down from the altar are busted by what looks like a crowbar that was thrown to the side and forgotten afterward. It doesn't look like there are any other rooms besides this one. My heart is pounding in my chest, to the point that I hear my own pulse. I want to shout 'hello' or something, but I don't want to alert anyone of my presence any more than I may already have.

On my way down from the high altar, I scan the floor for signs of a trap door or anything that would indicate a level below this one. There doesn't seem to be anything besides red pentagrams and other satanic symbols spray painted on the boards, some of which have rotted away. Bored teens or gang members clearly got in here before this place was locked up for good. I pick up the crowbar I saw earlier to have some sort of weapon inside this sacrilegious place.

Brooklyn, get out. Get the hell out of here right now.

The little voice in my head is nagging me to leave, and I can't deny how much I want to sprint out as fast as I can. The same uneasy feeling I got in Fraanco creeps up on me again, threatening to explode. I can see my breath in here more than I can outside. I want to wrap myself up in a blanket, watch a comforting movie, and forget I ever came here. My body can't stop moving as I fidget in place. In a desperate act, I open my mouth.

"Issac? Nicole?" I whisper. I don't know why I bother whispering since my voice echoes off the old slate stone anyway. A few more tense moments pass. There's no one here.

I turn around to leave and then take a step back. On the wall behind the altar, a massive crucifix is spray painted, blood coming out of its eyes and the words *HE SEES EVERYTHING* written behind it. *That's comforting.* My stomach flips over, the uneasiness crashing down on me. Now, I *really* want to leave. I make my way back up to the alter, planning to go through the window I entered, when I hear footsteps outside. There's nothing I can do as I watch two men come in through the window.

They're wearing black jackets, jeans, and work boots. They both have black bandanas wrapped around their heads. There's one with blonde hair and another with brown hair. Neither of them looks like the type of person I would want to meet alone. I gulp and hide the crowbar in my hand behind my legs. The man with lighter hair snickers.

"Well, well, who're you?" he snarls, sauntering down the altar with his cat-like eyes fixed on me. "Where'd you come from?" I open my mouth, but nothing comes out. I'm quickly regretting not having told anyone where I went. My grip on the crowbar tightens, so much so that I feel my fingernails digging into my palms as my hand clamps down harder.

"Not much of a talker," says the other. They step towards me, and I keep walking backwards down the center aisle, my boots cracking the glass beneath my feet. My knees have locked, so I stagger backwards like Frankenstein. "Pretty, though."

"You got a name, Pretty?" asks the first guy. My eyes search for another way to escape, but the two men are blocking the only exit. I walk slowly and try not to make any sudden movements, calculating a possible escape, like a cornered deer.

My back finally hits the front door of the church, chains rattling from the other side. When I slam against it, I swallow hard, watching the two of them prowl towards me. As they get closer, I notice the one with the lighter hair is missing two front teeth, and the other has sharpened all of his into points. *Great.* My stomach churns, and the blood racing through my ears is deafening. The man with the pointed teeth stops in front of me, and the other one stops to my left. I make sure to hide the crowbar between the back of my leg and the door. My palms ache, and I can't tell if my fingernails have drawn blood or if the moisture I feel is sweat. The man dons a twisted smile.

"Not talkative at all, are ya?" he says with a grin. He clicks his tongue disapprovingly. "You know, you're not supposed to be here, Pretty. Unless you got a death wish." The man looks at me with consideration. "Bleeker, you think she needs a tongue if she likes to talk this much?" The man with the lighter hair on the side of me shakes his head.

"Nah," says Bleeker.

"That's what I was thinkin' exactly," says the other man. He seizes the top of my head and pushes it back against the door, so he gets a better angle at my mouth. I seal my lips shut and breathe hard through my nose. He flicks open a switchblade. A whimper escapes through my lips. My eyes grow wider, and the man chuckles. "You picked the wrong day to come here, Pretty," he growls. He kicks me in the leg, I cry out, and he grabs onto my jaw to keep it open. Bleeker cackles as he puts his arm on my neck, and I try to struggle against it, but I choke.

"Whatcha want your last words to be, Pretty?" asks the guy to my side. "Want your boyfriend to help ya?" I attempt to shut my mouth, but I can't because the man's grip is like a vice, making sure I don't move whatsoever. When his knife is near my mouth, tears threaten to leak out of my eyes. Still, I have one last trick to use.

"Fuck you," I growl into the man's face.

Holding the crowbar behind my back like a baseball bat, I take aim at the man's legs. It hits him with a *crack*, and he automatically plummets to the floor, the knife skittering out of sight. Bleeker tries to clamp his hands around my neck, but I make the bar collide with his ribs and then with his crotch. Bleeker screams and staggers to the ground. While I'd like to take a second to gloat in victory, the other man gets up and punches me in the face. White spots speckle my vision as I stagger backwards from the force of the hit. I don't let go of the crowbar though, so when he goes to punch me again, I thrust it like a javelin into his ribcage. It slashes into his side, draws blood, and incapacitates him just enough for me to sprint back down the aisle, run up the altar, and jump through the broken window.

"GET BACK HERE!" roars Bleeker. Not heeding his demand whatsoever, I flat out sprint all the way back to the road, leaping over crumbled headstones and dodging tombs. My head is on a swivel. There might be more of them. When I see civilization, namely cars, I collapse onto the sidewalk and catch my breath. My chest heaves up and down as I look up to the sky. I don't think I've ever run so fast in my life. I put my hands together like Jared showed me and watch the clouds drift past peacefully.

"Thank you," I pant between breaths.

There's no way Nicole or Issac would be in that church unless the kidnapper was in that gang, but I highly doubt that. At least, I know they're not in the graveyard ... or in that *place* in the graveyard anyway.

When I get home, I go to the bathroom to remove my makeup, most of which has been wiped away by sweat. Looking in the mirror, it turns out, is a horrible idea. On my left cheekbone, I have a bruise the size of a fist that's getting darker by the minute. It's every shade of purple, blue, and black, with a tinge of green.

I gingerly wipe my face with a washcloth and barely touch the skin around the bruise. I lightly touch the black and blue bulge as I bite my bottom lip to keep myself from screaming. It aches badly. There must be something in this apartment I can use to keep the swelling down. The front door suddenly slams, so I quickly wipe away the rest of my makeup. I look down as I go back into my room, making sure to shield my face from my roommate.

"Hey, Brook," says Drew casually, going into her room. Ever the observer, she notices my odd walk. She stops in the hallway, takes a look at me, and exclaims, "What the hell is on your face?"

"Nothing. How was your day?" I ask, trying desperately to change the subject. Drew unceremoniously puts her bookbag in her room and comes back into the hallway, dragging me into the light. When she sees the bruise, she gasps.

"Holy *shit*, Brooklyn, where did you get that from?" she exclaims, horrified. I push my hair back from my face and hold my head high.

"I just fell, alright?"

"On your *face*?" Drew scoffs. "Brook, I'm smarter than that. I've taken a few hits in my life. That's what they look like. Where'd you get that from?"

"I fell in front of Rosenburg. It was icy. Will you stop?" I say sharply, going to sit on the couch in the living room.

"Brooklyn!" Drew says testily, sounding like a mother disappointed in her child's decisions. I sit down and cross my arms indignantly, looking up at her poignantly. "What's happening to you? Where did you go the other day? Is that where you got that monstrosity?"

"You really wanna know where I went yesterday?" I ask her. "Because you say that, then when I tell you, you're gonna freak out."

"Anything. Just tell me *something*." Drew sits down on the coffee table, leaning her elbows on her knees.

"You're scaring me a bit." Though I know she'll explode, in the end, it's best to tell her the truth, no matter what the consequences. I brace myself for the worst.

"I went to Ryker's house." Drew's expression drops. "And before you say anything—"

"Why the hell would you do that dumbass thing?" she condemns, looking at me in disbelief.

"I thought he might know something about the identity of Mask Man."

"And he hit you, why?"

"No, Ryker didn't hit me. I thought Issac was being held in the graveyard because when Kienan, Nate, and I went to the bus stop to look for clues, Kienan thought he heard a scream coming from the graveyard. I went there today, ran into some gang members, and barely got out in one piece. That's where I got this." I gesture to my ruined complexion. Drew runs a hand through her hair and looks around.

"Jesus. Alright, first thing's first. Why did you go to a bus stop to look for Issac?" I explain what transpired that night after the big argument. Drew seems satisfied with the details, so she continues with her interrogation. "Okay, so what happened with Ryker? First of all, I can't *believe* you visited that scumbag and trusted that he wouldn't trap you in his house," she scolds.

"His mom was home."

"Oh, thank *God*, 'cause that makes this *all* better," Drew sarcastically approves.

"You want to hear the story or not?" She begrudgingly stays silent, which I take as a cue to keep going. "I asked if he knew anyone still on campus, who had it out for me. Ryker said the cops sniffed out everyone that he knew of, so he didn't know who would be targeting me." Drew raises an eyebrow.

"And that's it? That's all that happened?" she pushes. She's good, I'll give her that. I nod.

"Yeah, that's it."

"Brook, you wouldn't go over there to ask *one* question. What else happened?" As soon as she finishes her sentence, her eyes grow wide. "Oh, no. You didn't ..."

"Didn't what?"

"You didn't hook up with him, did you?" I let out a bark of laughter.

"No, no, don't worry," I respond. Drew breathes a sigh of relief, but I still chew on my lip. "But he did ..." Drew's face becomes hard again.

"What did he do?" She sounds like she's going to kill someone.

"He asked me to let him help," I say. "And then we got really close, like forehead on forehead close. I think he was trying to kiss me." Drew explodes out of her seated position and jumps up onto the coffee table. Her fingers are pushing back her hairline. She's clearly disturbed by what I've just told her.

"And you *let him*?!" she shrieks.

"God, no!" Drew is so infuriated that she's finding it hard to speak. "Drew, it's fine! He's just—"

"He's just *what*?! *What*, Brooklyn?! Because the Brook *I* know would *never* let that piece of human garbage get anywhere *near* enough to try to kiss her!" I stand up as she paces two steps to either side of her on the coffee table.

"He's not garbage, Drew. He knows what he did was wrong—"

"Yeah, Brook, he *kidnapped* and tried to *kill* you. I would say that *more than* qualifies as wrong!"

"Drew, he tried to help me escape—"

138

"That was *after* he kidnapped you in his car, Brooklyn. God, if that guy kissed you, I would be over there right now." She slams her fist against her palm, vibrating with energy where she stands. She looks like she wants to angrily pace back and forth, but the coffee table is only a few feet long. "That complete jackass, who does he think he is?"

"Would you get down? You're scaring me." Drew rounds on me with big eyes.

"Am I? Am I *scaring* you? You got beat up by gang members, walked through a creepy cemetery *alone*, and *almost* cheated on your boyfriend, but *sure*, Brooklyn. *I* am scaring *you*." Her fingers are digging into her hips as her hands rest on her sides. I decide the best thing to do is to let her calm down. After fuming for a minute, Drew breaks into a little smile, snorting like she's figured it all out. She steps down from the table without looking where her foot is landing and shrugs. "It's so obvious, Brook. He's trying to seduce you to get what he wants."

"Drew, c'mon ..." I look at the wall and think back to the conversation I had with him a few nights ago. Ryker appeared to be lost. It seemed like he was holding onto *my* sanity to save himself. The look in his eyes said he wanted desperately to know what was going on outside the walls of his house. And how he successfully made me let him in on the investigation. All it took was some gazes of approval and talking in a low voice that triggered something in me.

I drop onto the couch and put my face in my hands, groaning and squeezing my eyes shut. I'm *such* an idiot. Drew smirks.

"Told you," she says, sounding like a five-year-old. "Look, I won't tell Nate about this. Whether or not you kissed him, he *hates* Ryker. Best you not tell him about it at all."

"I know," I tell her. Drew gestures to my bruise.

"Get some peas on that thing. You look like you had a bad night out." Pretending to laugh at her joke, I get up and search the freezer for an ice pack. I grab a bag of Kenni's frozen veggies and put it on my cheek. It's almost unbearably cold when it first touches my skin, but then it soothes the spot so much that I forget the initial pain.

"So, are you gonna keep him in the loop? 'Cause you know what I'm gonna say to that," sniffs Drew. I'm about to answer her when Finn bursts into the apartment. Without saying a word, he walks to the TV and turns it on.

"Finn, what the hell?" I ask him as he flips the channels around.

"Look," he says with a stony face as he lands on the channel he's looking for. It's the local news channel, with a young anchor behind the desk. She looks distressed even though she's not supposed to.

"And tonight, police are investigating the disappearance of yet another Resslar University student, Jared Quinn." I don't hear anything she says after that. I storm into my bedroom and slam the door. With my face buried in my pillow, I let out an ear-piercing scream.

Another student gone.

Ring ring. Ring ring.

I slowly walk over to my desk, where I see my phone ringing. Tentatively, I pick up the phone and put it to my ear. I stay silent and just hear breathing on the other end. There are already tears of distress in my eyes.

"What?" I ask tightly.

"You've heard." There it is. The augmented robotic voice I've heard in my nightmares.

"Of course, I have." I sit down on my floor with my back against the wall. "What do you want with me?"

"You need to pay for what you've done," says Mask Man.

"I brought those boys to justice," I defend.

"You brought chaos to campus. You need to pay." I hug my knees to my chest.

"Who are you taking next?" I ask, knowing the answer. Mask Man laughs.

"Then it wouldn't be fun for either of us." With the little willpower I have left, I go to stand by the window and lean on the sill as I look outside.

"I don't care what's *fun* for you," I snarl. "Release them. Now."

"You are not in the position to make demands."

"Come get me if you want. You know where I live."

"I do. That wouldn't be fun, though, would it?" There's a pause. "You look lovely tonight, by the way. Beautiful, actually."

The line goes dead.

I whirl around my room to find there's no one in it. My heart thumps loudly. I throw open the door to my closet and look inside. No one's there. The sudden urge to vomit overcomes me.

So *that's* how he knows when I'm home. He can somehow see into my room.

I can't sleep that night.

14

Covering up the bruise on my face with makeup takes me about a half hour the next morning. Throughout the day, I'm constantly ducking into the nearest bathroom to check if the bruise has poked through. This morning, I packed my powder, concealer, foundation, and even a little yellow circle under-eye correcting stick to negate some of the blue. Thankfully, all the products I caked on my face don't move.

I go to WRDW to finish up the work I left yesterday. Inside the building, it's nice and warm, which makes me want to catch up on sleep. However, I force myself to focus on my work. It's mundane, but it makes me feel better to see everyone I know. The station feels like a home more than ever, especially these days.

As I'm getting on the bus to go to my apartment, Nate calls. My entire body tenses. I triple-check the caller ID before picking it up.

"Hey, what's up?" I ask, trying to hide the tremble in my voice.

"Hey, what are you doing tomorrow night?" he says. Just as the bus starts to move, I grab onto the bar above my head to keep my balance. Everyone inside collectively sways backward as the bus accelerates.

"I don't think anything. Why? What's going on?"

"There's a DR party. Do you want to go?"

"Even with Jared and Issac gone?" I say in a pitiful voice.

"That's what I said, but Kienan says they'd want us to have the party."

"I think Kienan just *really* wants to get drunk," I laugh. Nate doesn't seem to hear the nervousness in my voice.

"I think that too, but it's nice to think the guys would want us to continue," Nate agrees. Though I'm not in the mood for a party, it beats sitting around my apartment and becoming mired in the new disappearances. Somewhat begrudgingly, I agree to it.

"Alright, I'll go. What time?"

"I'm getting on the bus at nine-ish. I'll pick you up before we go. Sounds good?"

"Yeah, sounds good."

"And if it's too much for you or if you're tired or something, I'd be more than happy to stay home and watch a bad movie," assures Nate. I grin.

"Same with you," I say. "If you don't want to be at the house, I understand." There's a pause, and the only thing we both hear is the bus engine groaning as it makes its way along the road. "How are you doing without Jared?"

"It's weird. It's like I keep expecting him to round a corner or walk through a door and be okay. I miss him more than I thought I could." We don't speak again until

143

he takes a deep breath as though he's trying to reset himself. "Mind if I come to your place tonight? I need to get away. Every time I look at Issac's room, I think of Jared, and it freaks me out."

"Understandable. I'm on the bus right now, but when I get home, you can come over." As soon as I say it, I remember the enormous bruise on my face. Well, can't take it back now.

"Awesome. See you in a few. Love you, babe."

"Love you too." Once I hang up, I politely shoulder my way off the bus and walk to my apartment in the bitter cold. I used to listen to music when I walked home, but now I'm too scared that someone will follow and jump me from behind.

It's quiet when I enter my apartment. I remember that Drew is going on a date with Finn tonight, and Kenni is at some debate for an organization she's in. I have the whole apartment to myself. When I think of that, my stomach starts to hurt with worry. Once I put on a pot of water for pasta, I go to my room to put my bag down. Of course, there's a little present for me waiting on my desk.

It's Jared's crucifix necklace, with a hand-written Post-It note next to it. The note reads: *NEXT TO.*

I'm too disgusted and disheartened to look at it a second longer. I put the crucifix on my chest of drawers, figuring I'll deliver it to Greenwood tomorrow. As I pour the pasta into the pot of hot water and stir absent-mindedly, I think about the victims.

The first was Nicole. She's a sophomore and Drew's friend. I knew her for all of two hours, and then she was taken. I had heard Drew talk about her before, and it sounded like the two of them were good friends, but I don't know why she'd be abducted. She seemed like a regular college student, non-offensive, just doing her best.

The next was Issac, also a sophomore and a Delta Rho brother. Kenni had a crush on him, and it didn't appear as though he was absolutely against her affections. He lived with Nate and was an engineering major. He seemed like a great guy and didn't have any enemies that I know of.

Now, there's Jared, an innocent freshman, a Delta Rho pledge, and Nate's fraternity little brother. Nate loved that kid like the brother he never had. Seems like all of Jared's praying got him nowhere.

There's no connection between any of them. If Nicole wasn't in the mix, I would think that Mask Man was targeting Delta Rho brothers, but that would hurt Nate more than it would hurt me. Mask Man wants me to pay for bringing the SHA guys to justice. Ryker said all underground frat brothers had been sniffed out and were not on campus anymore, but does Ryker have something to do with this? It's clear he still loves me, and he obviously still feels bad for kidnapping me last year. He did that to make Taylor happy, not out of his own free will. Taylor knew I was important to Ryker, and he took advantage of that to get to me—

Wait.

I stop stirring the pot and go to my room, taking out index cards from my desk. I quickly scribble down the names of the people who were taken and the names of the people they were important to. Then, I roll up little pieces of tape and stick each card on the inside of my closet door to hide them from Mask Man, in case he gets in my room again. When I line each of their names up, it makes sense.

Nicole is important to Drew.

Issac is important to Kenni.

Jared is important to Nate.

Mask Man has taken people close to the people I love. Drew, Kenni, Nate ... He's missing Finn ...

Who's important to Finn?

"Brook?" Nate asks from the living room. I quickly shut the closet door and leave my room to go hug my boyfriend. "Oh, there you are! I wasn't sure if I should come in."

"Yeah, you're good. I was just changing," I lie, going back to the stove and turning off the electric burner. I quickly drain the water out of the pasta and dump some red sauce into the pan. "Do you want pasta?"

"If you have extra, I'll take some." Nate leans in the doorway to the kitchen and watches me prepare dinner. I make sure to keep my head down. When I go to pick up the bowls, Nate puts them back down and kisses me. Something inside me melts as he kisses me harder and deeper. We stand there for a good fifteen seconds before I pull away and look at him with a suspicious face.

"What was that about?" I ask him.

"I just haven't kissed you in a while. Makes me feel better about the shit going on," he says, looking into my eyes with worry. When he searches my face, I know I should turn away, but it's too late. He's spotted the bruise. His eyebrows shoot up as his jaw drops. I glance up at him.

"What?" I ask innocently. Nate goes to touch my face and I involuntarily flinch.

"*Brooklyn,* what the *hell* is on your cheek?" he whispers as his eyes widen. I step backward as though retreating will fix the fact that my makeup has finally rubbed off.

"Nate—"

"Where'd you get that? Did someone hit you? I swear to God, if someone hit you, I'll—"

"Nate, calm down!" I exclaim as I see the fire in his eyes ignite. "I'll tell you what happened if you promise to stay calm."

"I can't promise anything." I take a measured breath out through my nose.

"Alright, so I went into the graveyard the other night to see if I could find where they were keeping Issac and Nicole and—" I can see him getting ready to interrupt me, and I give him a pointed look to shut him up. He fights with himself to stay put. "I went into that creepy church in the back of the graveyard, by the train tracks, alongside the highway, and I had a run-in with two gang members. When I was escaping, one of them punched me."

"You went into the graveyard *at night alone*? When you know full well that all this shit is going on?" Nate utters in disbelief.

"Well, it was light outside when I went in but turning dark when I came out."

"That typically happens during the day," Nate grimaces.

"Look, they're not in there. At least, I found that out."

"Why did you even look in there?"

"Because Kienan said he heard screams coming from there the night Issac was taken," I defend. Nate pinches the bridge of his nose with his fingers. It's as though I've disappointed my mother, which I despise doing. There's no pleasure in telling him any of this, and I can tell he's trying not to explode. Finally, he speaks, albeit stiffly.

"Alright, I get it. Just promise me when you're going somewhere like that in the future, you tell me, and I'll come. If you get kidnapped, there's no one else on this campus that Mask Man talks to. I'll have to pick up the slack," Nate jokes. I smile at him, taking my bowl of pasta and sitting at the table. He follows suit.

"Deal." The two of us chew in silence until he talks again.

"You know, the other day Kienan was going through Issac's stuff just to see if he could find something," Nate starts. "He found this sheet of paper that was just Kenni's name over and over, with either the word 'yes' or 'no' in front of it." He smiles faintly. "It was cute, but kinda creepy."

"So Issac liked Kenni?"

"*Likes*. Let's not use past tense until we know for certain he's dead."

"True. But he has a crush on her?"

"I think so ... Issac doesn't talk about his feelings that much. No guy really does. I mean, you're around the guys all the time, I'm pretty much the only guy in my frat in touch with my feelings," jokes Nate.

"I don't get why more guys don't show their soft side. Girls like that kind of stuff," I comment with a mouth full of pasta.

"It's just easier to be a robot. Especially now, when everyone is disappearing. The guys think one of them will be next."

I don't tell him that I think it's a possibility.

^^^

"Hey, Brooklyn," says Ryker smoothly over the phone that night. I'm standing at my closet door, looking at the index card chart I've made. I can tell by the way he's speaking that he's smiling. "Found anything new?"

"Yeah, actually."

"What?" he asks eagerly, practically cutting me off in desperation.

"How do I know you're not with them like you were last time?" I question. Ryker scoffs.

"Because they hate me now that I helped you. C'mon Brook, tell me what's going on." I lean against my closet door, looking at the floor and studying the flecks of color among the beige weave.

"Ryker, I can't just *tell* you things, especially not over the phone." *Let's see if I can get an invite this time instead of showing up unannounced.* Ryker seems angrily confused.

"What do you want from me?"

"I want you to tell me everything you know about SHA."

"And what do I get?"

"I tell you about the investigation."

"Brooklyn, if I'm going to fully betray that fraternity, they're going to come after me one way or another. I need something else." He's right technically. Once the brothers realize that I know every little detail about their world and Ryker was the one who told me, they're going to murder him. "So, what do you want to give me, Brooklyn?" My nose twitches in annoyance.

"Nothing. You're not in a position to make demands, Ryker. With all you've done to me, this is the *least* you can do," I spit. I hear him chuckle on the other end.

"You're not wrong. I'm imagining you want to talk in person?"

"Can you meet two days from now? It's a Sunday." I hear Ryker flip through a book.

"Let me check. Oh, look I'm free," he deadpans.

"Tell your mom I'm coming this time," I remind him.

"Alright. See you Sunday, Brooklyn Perce."

"Bye." I hang up the phone and toss it lightly onto my bed, gnawing on my thumbnail but not chewing it off entirely. I still need some nail left if I want to have a form of self-defense.

15

The next night, Nate and I arrive at the Delta Rho house party. It's not as loud as usual, and I assume that's because two of their own are missing. Inside, the house smells like stale body odor, cheap beer, and Axe cologne. Despite the lower volume, it's packed inside since it's one of the only houses open tonight, and most of the prospective pledges for the spring semester are here.

After hanging around the bar for much of the night, I discover I'm nicely drunk. I talk to people about random things since my brain can't really process much at the moment. Eventually, I see someone I know. Andy Nyall is a smaller freshman whose nerdy looks truly match his intellect. I would be surprised if his IQ weren't over 140. Andy's normally quiet, but he can't shut up after a few beers. He smiles at me when our eyes meet and lets the foam from the keg drip down the side of his red cup.

"Hiya, Brooklyn! How are you?" he asks.

"I'm doing great, Andy! What about you? Finishing up your first semester alright?" I pour vodka and cranberry juice into a cup, guessing the measurements, and take a swig, smacking my lips at the gross taste of the flavored vodka.

"Yeah, it's just a lot more work than I thought it would be. I can handle it though." He happily pushes up his glasses on his nose and sips his beer. When another brother walks up to us, Andy quickly swallows his beer and straightens up. I identify the new brother as Walt Springfield, another freshman who rushed this semester and was accepted with flying colors. He has close-cut darker hair, which matches his eyes. He would seem handsome to someone like Drew and clearly to someone like Andy, who clears his throat.

"Hey, 'sup, Andy? 'Sup, Brooklyn?" asks Walt nonchalantly.

"Nothing. What's going on with you?" I respond politely. Andy seems to have forgotten how to speak, so I gently nudge him with my elbow, and he remembers.

"H-hey, Walt," he says weakly. Walt smiles and then grabs a beer out of the crowded fridge. I spy some moldy leftovers and more twelve packs.

"Well, I'll leave you two alone," I say, realizing that Andy is getting flustered. "I'll see you later."

I make my way through the crowded house to the second floor and find Nate chatting with Kienan and some other brothers. This is where they always go to get away from the commotion downstairs. They have cups in their hands and seem like they should be having fun, but their expressions indicate otherwise. When I approach, they greet me with half-hearted smiles.

"Hey, you." Nate puts his arm around my waist and kisses me on the head. I nestle into his blue DR sweatshirt and give him a half hug.

"Hey. What are we talking about?"

"Just wonderin' how Jared's doin' wherever he is," says a black-haired brother glumly.

"He's fine," reassures Kienan as he sips his beer.

"No, he's not. That guy's dead," says a familiar voice. When I adjust myself, I see Brendon among the brothers. I didn't spot him before since his skinny frame is easy to miss. He's sitting on a beat-up leather armchair with a Bud Light in one hand and his other hand lazily draped off the arm. "Not trying to be a downer, but it's probably true." He looks up at me and shrugs as if to say *what can you do?*

"Why did we include him in this conversation?" a blonde-haired guy asks, with a laugh. The other guys chuckle along in agreement.

"I'm being realistic," says Brendon, standing up and stopping their laughter. "The first one was kidnapped, what? A week and a half ago? She's probably dead." My unsettled feeling must be evident on my face because Kienan speaks up.

"Brendon, c'mon, dude. Shut up," Kienan pushes after he sees how shaken I look.

"You gonna catch the guy again?" asks Brendon as if he didn't hear, turning and looking at me expectantly. I can't help but notice the condescending tone in his voice. "You gonna swoop in and save the world?"

"Trying to," I say tightly. "And for the record, when the guys kidnapped me and chucked me in a closet, they wanted to kill me, but one of them wouldn't let the others. Nicole and Issac and Jared are alive." Brendon sips his beer.

"Oh really? Which one didn't want to kill you?" asks Brendon.

"Ryker Williams. The leader."

"Wait, I've heard that name before," says the black-haired brother. He looks at Nate. "Was that the guy you fought with a sword?"

"No, that was the one who wanted to kill me. Taylor," I correct.

"Ryker's the guy who liked Brook. Emphasis on the past tense there," Nate says, trying to joke but failing. "How's he doing by the way, Brook? Do you know?"

"He's fine. Looks horrible, but he's fine." Nate takes his arm off my hip and slowly turns to me. I bite my bottom lip out of annoyance with myself and my loose tongue. *Why did I mention Ryker's looks?* Brendon sits back down and looks at me with a knowing smile. The other brothers have fallen silent, including Kienan, who's now interested in guzzling his beer.

"How do you know how he *looks*?" Nate asks slowly, his eyebrows furrowing. I flounder for a second as my intoxicated brain clumsily figures out my next move. *I saw him on Instagram, someone posted a photo with him, say* anything!

"I mean ... I *assume* he looks horrible," I quickly say, trying to cover my drunken tracks, but it's too late.

"When would you have *seen* him?" Nate questions. He's growing angrier by the second. Brendon's beer is halfway to his mouth as a knowing smile overtakes his face. The brothers around us have paused as well. They want to see how this pans out.

"Nate, please don't," I mutter, looking around and reaching out to him with a shaky hand.

"Brooklyn, have you ... have you *seen* Ryker?" His eyes search my face as I try not to look guilty. When I don't deny it, he shakes his head, looking horrified. Nate yanks his hand away from mine and storms off.

"Well done," Brendon comments mockingly, breaking the silence and sipping his beer again. I put my drink down and leave the room, running down the stairs and pushing my way through drunk and dancing people. Nate's nowhere to be found. I check by the bar and just barely catch the back door clicking shut.

When I burst outside, the frigid air hits my face immediately and starts freezing my wet eyelashes. The beads of sweat on my face also turn to ice on impact. I lightly jog to the front of the house and look both ways down the sidewalk. Sure enough, Nate has taken a left and is walking towards campus. Although I don't want to move, I force myself to run after him. I can feel the alcohol weighing on my stomach, and I get the sensation that I need to vomit when I reach him. I tug on his sleeve, and he turns around. He's very angry. I don't need to be sober to tell that. The air around him is ignited with his hatred. We stand there just staring at each other, wondering who will budge first.

"When did you see him?" Nate finally asks tightly.

"A few days ago."

"Was he the one who hit you?" he says through his teeth.

"No. No, the man at the graveyard hit me." Nate scoffs.

"So why did you go to him?"

"I thought he would have something to tell me about the kidnappings."

"And did he?" I look at my feet. "*Did he?*" Nate repeats insistently.

155

"No."

"So, you went to his house, without telling anyone, to try to get information that you ended up not getting?" Nate recounts. He shakes his head in shame, his fingers threatening to close into fists at his sides. I stay quiet, fearing that I may say something I don't mean. "Brook, do you trust me?"

"Of course, I—"

"No, you don't. If you did, you would've told me about the graveyard, about Ryker, about all of it, right when it happened." I step closer to him.

"Nate—"

"Brooklyn, you seem to forget that someone wants to *kill* you *again*! I don't doubt you can handle yourself, but with this shit going on, you gotta tell someone where you're going because, one day, you're not going to come back," Nate chides. On one hand, I'm furious with him. He doesn't own me, nor does he get to dictate where I can and can't go, but I'm silent because I know he's right. Maybe my dad had a point when he said I treat my life with troubling casualty. "Did anything else happen that I should know about?"

"Ryker, when I saw him, he ..." Nate's lips become a thin line, and his eyes widen. "He tried to kiss me."

"*What?*" Nate just mouths the word. He's too shocked to say anything.

"Nate, he didn't, he wanted to, but—"

"That fucking *snake!*" Nate yells, finally breaking his ridged pose and pacing in a circle once. There's a fire in his amber eyes that I wish I hadn't lit. "I'm gonna kill that fucking guy. I swear to God. I'm gonna murder his smug ass. Should've taken the sword to him instead of Taylor." He starts muttering to himself how he's going to kill Ryker, seeming to forget I'm standing there trembling. There are tears threatening to emerge from my eyes. He looks like someone told him his entire family was lost in an accident: angry, sad, and confused.

"Nate, I'm—"

"I've always been there for you. Through everything. You're my girlfriend, I love you. And now…" It sounds like he's talking to himself, irate and annoyed. Finally, he collects himself, but his hands are in fists at his sides. "I'm going home. You look freezing. Go back to the house to get warm." He starts walking away.

"Nate!" I call. He turns around. "I'm so, so sorry."

"You're drunk. Go back to the house, Brooklyn," Nate says. He flips his hood up and then walks away from me, leaving me in the cold.

^^^

Back inside the house, I sprint upstairs, lock myself in the bathroom, sit on the closed toilet bowl, and start to cry. Tears stream down my face, and I don't know if it's because of the copious amount of alcohol in my system or the fact that every emotion I've ever bottled up is now spilling out. I feel like I was kicked in the stomach then punched across the face. The one thing I thought was solid in my life, and I've gone and ruined it for a second time. Unlike the last instance, I don't think this can be fixed.

I hear the door open and look up to see the newcomer while quickly wiping my running mascara. To my surprise, it's Gavin. He sees me and looks unsure as to what he's walked into.

157

"Oh, um, sorry," he mumbles, trying to smile to ease the tension. The process of getting to my feet is slow, but I get there, still wiping the messy makeup from my face.

"No, it's fine. I was just leaving actually," I say, my voice attempting to be strong. Gavin nods and watches me rip a square of toilet paper from the roll to blot my face. I look in the mirror at my puffy eyes and fix myself up. He's still standing awkwardly in the doorway, so I figure I might as well make conversation if he insists on staying. "What brings you to the house?"

"This house is one of the only ones open tonight. They don't usually let guys in, but I know people here. Thinking about rushing next semester," Gavin answers honestly. He gestures at my face with the hand holding a beer bottle. "You need help there?"

"No, thanks. I'll be okay." I sniff in and square my shoulders, trying to act like I didn't just have a breakdown in a grimy frat house bathroom.

"What are you so upset about?" he says.

"Nothing," I mutter, wiping mascara from underneath my eyes.

"Know what I think?" he asks. I don't answer since I don't care what he thinks. Regardless, he tells me anyway. "I think you're unnecessarily crying."

"Oh, yeah? I can't cry 'cause I just lost my boyfriend? I'm not allowed to cry for that?" I loudly retort, a pissed look overtaking my face. Gavin's eyes widen.

"Damn. Didn't realize it was that bad," he apologizes.

"It's been constantly bad ever since last year. This is par for the course at this point." I sigh and look at myself in the mirror, trying to decide if I like the girl who's staring back. "I never thought I'd hurt him like that. I'm a *horrible* person, Gavin. I'm a miserable, horrible, toxic person." I start to take shaky breaths like I'm going to cry again. Gavin finally decides to come into the bathroom and shuts the door behind him.

"Hey, hey, look at me. Look at me, Brooklyn," Gavin says, putting his beer down on the toilet tank. I look up at him as little tears trickle down my face again. "You're a great person, alright? Probably one of the best on the campus. Hell, you solved one of the—"

"God, will people *stop talking* about that?" I exclaim, crying harder. "People won't stop telling me how noble it was that I broke that case. I'm not a goddamn *hero*! I'm not some icon or idol! I'm a 19-year-old, who was almost *murdered* and got lucky. And now I'm cursed 'cause as long as I'm alive, they're gonna keep coming after me." I look defiantly at him. "I should've just died in the basement of that house like I was supposed to." When I say that, Gavin looks scared.

"Don't say that, Brooklyn. That's not you talking, that's the alcohol."

"You don't know me, Gavin! You've met me twice, and the first time we met, I got a bad feeling about you." Gavin snorts.

"Makes sense. I seem to scare a lot of people when I initially meet them," he considers. "But, Brooklyn, just because you're having this *one* moment of doubt shouldn't drive you to want to be dead." Though he's trying to make me feel better, I don't want the consolation.

"You don't understand. The kidnappings are for *me*, Gavin. As some sick revenge for bringing SHA to justice. Some asshole on this campus still wants me to find them and die for what I've done." His eyes widen. "I'm being threatened again, and this guy is dead set on slitting my throat in front of the entire campus if that's what it takes." In exasperation, I sit down on the closed toilet and throw up my hands. "I don't even know why I'm here. The guy could be watching me." My head finds a home in my hands as Gavin lets the information sink in.

"Wow," he finally says.

"And I need my boyfriend now more than ever, and he just ..." I try to hold back tears again. "He just left me here. And he knows what's going on."

"That's so shitty," agrees Gavin. He squats down, so he's eye level with me like a father consoling his child. "Look, I don't want to pretend I know what you're going through because I clearly don't. So, here's what I'm going to do. We're going to call you an Uber and get you home, alright? Is someone home when you get there?"

"Drew should be," I quietly say with a sniffle.

"Okay, good. When you get home, I want you to drink water and calm yourself down. Here, do you have my number?" My head drunkenly swings from side to side in an exaggerated head shake. Digging in my pocket, I find my phone and hand it to him. "Okay, here. Text me when you get home. Let's get you downstairs, alright?" I nod like a child, and he helps me stand.

We go downstairs, where everything is too loud and bright. I push past Brendon and Kienan and other party goers who don't seem to care that my world just shattered. Kienan offers to help me out, but Gavin waves him away. Luckily, there's an Uber passing by the house when Gavin orders one, so I go straight from the house to the interior of the car. Gavin helps me inside and shuts the door, reminding me one more time to text him when I get home. As we drive away, I close my eyes and lean my head back on the seat. The silence of the car is a relief to my ears that are tired of processing sound.

The Uber drops me off in front of my apartment building and drives away. When I enter my unit, I go to the kitchen and down two glasses of tap water, wiping my lips with the back of my hand when I'm through. What little of my lipstick is left smears on my skin, leaving a reddish mark. I lean on the counter and take a few deep breaths, taking in the familiar smell of home. Calming myself down has gotten harder since last year. I've made my peace with the fact that I'll never be a hundred percent stress-free. I text Gavin that I've arrived and then put my phone back in my pocket.

"Drew?" I call, though my voice is tired. When I get no reply, I perk up in interest. "Drew, you okay?" Another pregnant pause. I nudge open the door to her room and am greeted by a blast of cold air from the outside. Quickly, I run to the window and shut it. The fairy lights that go around the perimeter of her room are on, and her laptop is open on her desk. Her bed is still made, and her backpack is on the floor. Her phone is nicely placed on her desk next to the laptop bag.

The only thing Drew's room is missing is Drew.

Oh, no ...

"DREW!" I scream, running to the end of the hallway to check in Kenni's room and the bathroom. No one is in this apartment but me. I go into my room to make sure that there aren't any clues in there. I open the closet door and find there's been an addition to my chart. Under the index cards for Drew, Kenni, and Nate, there is a new one with the word *FINN*, written in red Sharpie. Across from his card is Drew's name. A whimper escapes me. I frantically rip my phone out of my pocket and call Kenni's number. She picks up on the fourth ring.

"Hey, Brook, what's—"

"Have you seen Drew?" I ask wildly.

"No, she wasn't home when I went out," says Kenni. A chill creeps up my spine, and I start walking in circles in the hallway. "Brooklyn? Brooklyn, what's going on?"

"Kenni, I think they got Drew," I whisper. Kenni doesn't respond.

"I'm coming home." She hangs up abruptly, and I slowly shut the closet door, turning to look at my desk.

I want to collapse to the floor and sob all over again.

On the desk, I see a nicely folded royal blue sweatshirt with the Delta Rho letters stitched into it. I know that sweatshirt all too well. I pick it up and hug it to my chest. Underneath it, I see two more index cards. In a goopy red liquid, my name is written on one of the cards, and the other has Nate's name on it. When I remove a hand from the sweatshirt, I find that the liquid has covered my fingertips, and, God, does it stink.

I think I'm going to throw up and faint at the same time.

Ring ring. Ring ring.

I answer the phone.

"BROOKLYN! BROOKLYN, PLEASE HELP ME! BROOKLYN, HELP!" screeches Nate. I'm silent as I stand there in horror. I feel like I've been stabbed in the stomach. This isn't real. It can't be. I'm in a dream. I must be. He keeps screaming and then is choked off. I say nothing.

The line clicks even though Mask Man didn't say a word.

The silence in the apartment crushes my eardrums.

16

Sunday morning begins with birds singing outside of my window. I don't know why they're so happy or what they're singing about when the world is falling apart.

When I finally muster up the energy to get out of bed and walk down the hallway, I find Kenni in the kitchen, making breakfast. She looks at me with a thin smile.

"I called the police, this morning, about Drew. They said they'll—"

"Conduct a campus-wide search as soon as possible," I easily fill in, sitting down at the table with a slouch. "It's what they all say. Meanwhile, Drew, Issac, and the others are probably out in Northwich somewhere dying."

"You can't think like that," Kenni says, putting a plate of eggs in front of me. "Made these for you. I don't know if you're hungry though." The smell of the eggs, which normally would be welcomed, just makes me nauseous. I put my hands inside of the sleeves of Nate's sweatshirt. I slept in it last night as some sick way to feel closer to my kidnapped boyfriend. "What did Nate have to say?"

"Nate's gone too," I whisper. Kenni drops her fork on her plate and looks at me in disbelief.

"You're *kidding*," she gapes. "They got Drew *and* Nate last night? God, they work quickly."

"I got drunk last night. I didn't realize they would take advantage of that. Clearly, I underestimated them. Knew I shouldn't have gone to that stupid party." I poke at the eggs with my fork. They fall apart when I prod them, and the smell only intensifies. "Hey, have you told Finn yet?"

"Told me what?" Finn always has perfect timing. He comes into our apartment and puts his backpack down. "I have a study date with Drew. Where is she?" Kenni and I exchange a look across the table. After a staring battle, I lose. I turn around in my chair and take a deep breath.

"Finn, Drew was kidnapped last night," I say softly. Finn is paralyzed. "And no one knows where she is." Finn leans back against the wall and slowly sinks down. He hits the ground, stares straight ahead, and doesn't speak. Slowly, tears begin to emerge from his eyes, and I watch my friend crumble there on the carpeted floor. He puts his face in his hands and cries harder. Kenni gets up and goes over to him, putting one arm around his shoulder and leaning her head against his. She looks up at me as if to say *he was going to find out eventually*.

"It's okay Finn. They'll find her. It'll be okay, you'll see," Kenni consoles. I stand up from the table and go back into my room. I don't want to watch Finn cry. It'll just make me feel worse. After shutting the door, I pull on a pair of jeans but leave Nate's sweatshirt on. My hair is still in a messy ponytail, so I take it out but don't bother brushing it. It looks fine in its loose curls from last night. I glance at myself in the mirror on my desk to see if I need any makeup. That's when I notice something bizarre.

There's a small black box sitting on top of the mirror, no bigger than my pinky nail. When I pick it up, I can see a little red light coming from the bottom and a tiny camera lens in front.

It's a camera.

So *that's* how Mask Man knows when I'm not home.

I crush it beneath my foot until I hear a satisfying cracking sound. Who knows how many more of these things are in my room or in the apartment? There could be one in every space in this house. I don't want to think about it. I already have an unpleasant task to do today.

Out in the living room, Kenni is talking to Finn in a low tone on the couch. He has stopped crying, but his eyes are red and puffy. I can still see the tracks left by tears on his cheekbones.

"Where are you going?" Kenni asks me.

"Doing research. Hey, if you feel up to it, go around the apartment and look for these little black box things. They're about the size of a fingernail and have a red light. If you find any of them, crush them." I open the front door and take one last look at Finn. "I'm going to find Drew. I promise, Finn." Finn nods and tries for a smile, but it can't seem to form.

^^^

The Uber drops me off in front of Ryker's house around noon. Other than his beat-up Saturn which probably won't be driven for another few months, I don't see any cars in the driveway.

I knock on the door and try to prepare myself for what might happen once I enter this house. Ryker could've double-crossed me and told the former SHA guys that we were meeting. They could kidnap me and torture me to their hearts' content. Or it could just be Ryker and his cunning self. Thankfully, it's the latter case when he opens the door.

"Hey," he greets when he sees me. He has sort of trimmed his beard for the occasion and has on a grey t-shirt and sweatshirt with jeans. It reminds me of the days I saw Ryker at the radio station under happier circumstances.

"Hi." I enter the house, and he shuts the door behind me, making a sound like he's displeased with the cold.

"It's days like today that I'm thankful I can't go outside," Ryker jokes weakly. He looks around the corner to the kitchen and then nods. "Let's go to my room, yeah? Mom's at the supermarket, but if she comes home and sees you, she's going to actually kill me." I don't say anything and just follow him upstairs. This entire visit feels like a mistake. And to be wearing Nate's sweatshirt is like a slap in the face both to him and Ryker.

Ryker's room is again clean. There are a few library books on the desk that were absent the last time, but, other than that, everything is the same. I lean against his chest of drawers, thinking it's best if I stay as far away from the bed as possible. He, however, sits on the mattress and looks me up and down.

"You don't look so well," he says.

"Fantastic observation," I unintentionally snap, looking at the floor.

"Did they take someone else?"

"Drew." Ryker does a low whistle.

"Your roommate, right? Jesus," he mutters when I nod. He bites his bottom lip as though he's trying to contain himself. "But there's someone else, right?" I look into his eyes. He knows Nate is missing. He just wants to hear me say it. There's a smugness in his eyes that makes the sick feeling in my stomach grow.

"Nate. They got Nate," I admit. Ryker stands and puts his hands in his pockets.

"And *there* it is," he smirks. "That's why you're acting all moody. Your boyfriend is missing. Damn shame."

"Shut the hell up," I retort loudly. He's taken aback by the tone of my voice and sits back down.

"Alright, so you're here. What do you want to know?"

"A lot of shit."

"Fire away." Ryker settles into his seat and makes an open gesture with his hands. I'm not here to waste his time or mine, so I dive in.

"Those boys in the fraternity. Why were they there?" Ryker thinks for a second, then launches into his answer.

"Two reasons. The most common one was they felt like outcasts. They were either rejected from their top fraternity, or they didn't feel like they were a part of the frat they were in. The other reason was one of their relatives was in SHA before them. That was my case. My half-brother, Mitch, was in the fraternity the year it was cited then banned. He always told me stories about it, and it sounded like a lot of fun. I didn't really like any of the other frats and SHA felt like home." I raise my eyebrows.

"You have a half-brother?" Ryker sighs and nods, looking at the floor.

"Yeah. I used to talk to him all the time, but he's about 20 years older than me, so it's hard to keep in touch. My dad, he ... wasn't loyal to anyone, hence the half-brother before he and my mom met. It's always been my mom and me. We only have each other. My dad was never part of my life, and it was only a few years ago that I found out I had Mitch, so ..." He trails off, starting to look uncomfortable. I put him back on track.

"You seemed to have power over Taylor. Why was that?"

"Mitch was president of the fraternity back in his day. Since the frat was mainly underground, we had to establish some rules, and one of them was legacies always got priority, which helped keep membership relatively low. So, because Mitch was president, I got to be president too. And, to be honest, I fit the bill pretty well. I was a senior, I was heavily involved on campus, I was well-liked, I was basically the definition of a good president. Taylor bullied his way up to the vice presidency, and when he found out I had offered to help you bust the frat, as you remember, he dethroned me because it was in his right, plus he had been wanting to do that for some time."

"What did you guys do before you decided to hunt me?"

"Nothing, really. We would meet every so often and just chill. It felt nice to have a place where we belonged, you know? Everyone wants a family, and, for a lot of us, those guys were it. It was purely a social thing, nothing malicious behind it. It was cool to have a secret, and it was fun to go against the school in some way." I bite my bottom lip in contemplation.

"So, when did it turn into the 'Let's Kill Brooklyn' club?" I ask after a pause. Ryker pushes himself off the bed and begins to walk over to me.

"You *really* want to get into this?" he exhales.

"Yeah, I really do." I put a hand on his chest and gently shove him away from me. He chuckles under his breath as though he was expecting me to do so. "Talk, Williams."

"Alright, so you asked me, that one night in my car, about the house. You seemed like you were going to look into it, so James called you and warned you to stay away from it. The guys got skittish after that. They were afraid someone was going to find them out, that they were going to get expelled, or you were going to tell the cops. So, after James called, most of the guys went into survival mode, with Taylor leading the charge. He already hated you, so it was only natural that he wanted to be the one to stop you. They watched your every move, got pictures on their phones to track where you were and when, so if you did anything out of the ordinary, we would know. And then you told Drew, so we put guys on her, and then you told Nate, so we put guys on him. Everything they did from the night you mentioned the house to me onward was purely out of fear."

"And you say 'they' like you weren't involved. Weren't you the president? Shouldn't they have done what you said?" Ryker scoffs.

"You would think so. I kept saying you would eventually drop it, but the more I said that, the more you dug into the case. Eventually, the guys became suspicious of me. I didn't realize someone had stolen my WRDW pass and bugged the station, so when I offered to help you, they knew and totally stopped listening to me at that point. They followed Taylor then. Once you got those guys going, they didn't stop. They wanted to defend the brotherhood. It didn't matter that they were going to end up murdering an innocent, curious girl. They just wanted to save their family."

"Taylor wanted to kill me from the get-go?"

"Yeah, he wanted you out of the equation. The vendetta that he had against you, combined with the one he had against Nate for not getting into Delta Rho, just made him want to kill you more. There was a point where he was trying to convince the guys to kill Nate too, but they didn't go for it. They realized that Nate was being sucked into your investigation, and you were leading the charge. Taylor just wanted blood, and he didn't care who he got it from." I pinch the bridge of my nose with my fingers, trying to process the information thrown at me. Ryker is silent.

"So, how did you get tasked with kidnapping me if you were against all of this?" I finally question. Ryker swallows, his eyes darting around as though he's looking for an escape in his own home.

"On Halloween, when you came to the station and left Drew and Dexter alone, Dex got Drew drunk on Taylor's orders. She started going on about you and how you were so close to cracking the case. Dexter called me and Taylor, and we devised a plan. You just happened to be in my care at the time." When I don't say anything, Ryker comes back over to me and looks remorsefully at me. "I never wanted to hurt you, much less kill you. You gotta understand that." Ryker gently pushes my hair out of my face and tucks it behind my ear. "We were both in the wrong place at the wrong time."

"As always," I mutter. I walk around the other side of his bed and out of his reach, processing everything. The photos hanging on the walls aren't particularly interesting to me, but I pretend they are to avoid looking at him. A question that had formed in the back of my mind earlier suddenly comes to the surface.

"Ryker," I say, turning back to him. "What were you going to do with me after you … after you killed me?" He grimaces like I've just said the most painful thing on the planet.

"Brooklyn …"

"Tell me," I order in a soft voice, not sure I want to know the answer. He appears as though he's recalling one of the worst memories of his life. Finally, he slowly starts.

"Taylor wanted to leave you in the basement to rot. He hoped something would eat you, I guess. Actually, a few of the guys wanted to leave you there. I think they were just following his lead."

"And you? What did you want to do with me?" I ask. Ryker gulps, takes a measured breath, runs a hand through his hair, and keeps looking around. I'm grateful he has to take some time to think about what he's done. A part of me wants to run home and never think about this ever again. The same curiosity that brought me into this mess in the first place keeps me rooted to the spot.

"I couldn't just leave you there. The thought of something eating you made me sick. I wanted to bury you in the cemetery, by the train tracks. Maybe mark your grave somehow, I don't know. I didn't want you to be lost forever. I wanted someone to have at least a chance of finding you. I couldn't help but think of your parents, your friends … your boyfriend … crying their eyes out because your body couldn't be found. I wanted to give you a proper burial, but Taylor took over. So, I'd imagine if they killed you, they would've just left you there." I'm stunned. Ryker shakes his head, and I notice he's trying not to cry. "Sometimes, I have nightmares that we kill you," he whispers. "You plead with me not to hurt you. You say that you'll stay away from the case if we don't hurt you. It doesn't matter. They all end the same." We stand in silence for a while, both of us holding back tears. His are tears of remorse, and mine are tears of shock.

I feel nothing for him. He's a horrible person no matter how much he wants my sympathy. Drew was right: Ryker can repent all he wants, but, at the end of the day, he still threw away any shred of friendship or trust we had when he kidnapped me. For once, I see Ryker through Nate's eyes, and an odd mix of anger, disappointment, and sadness boils inside me. I believed in Ryker to a disastrous point, so when it turned out he was the opposite of everything I thought he was, everything came crashing down in a destructive wave, washing me out, leaving me tired and alone.

"I swear, if it wasn't for Taylor, none of this would've happened," Ryker says, toughening up and crossing his arms to prove it.

"I wish I never met him," I say.

"Even if you two never met, he'd still want to kill you." I stare at Ryker as he looks out of the window as the wind shakes the glass. "He thinks you're better than him, and he can't have that. So, naturally, he'd rather destroy you than live with his sense of inferiority."

17

Monday classes come and go, with me not saying a word to anyone. I've retreated into myself, only speaking when spoken to and walking around like a ghost, praying to God that no one recognizes or approaches me. I keep thinking about what Ryker told me yesterday and how that bastard Taylor wanted to kill me without a second thought. The more I think about him behind bars, the happier I become. He's dangerous and would've probably choked me to death that night in the frat house if he wasn't stopped.

Finn comes over to our apartment that afternoon and does his homework in silence in Drew's room. When I came home from Ryker's house yesterday, that's where I found him. He was just lying on her bed, looking up at the ceiling and every so often tilting his head to the side and gazing at the photos on her wall. I knew better than to disturb him. When I asked Kenni what Finn was doing, she told me that he told her that sitting in Drew's room made him feel less lonely. I didn't question it after that.

"Hey, Finn, I'm going to make chicken. Do you want some?" I offer after I put my bag down in my room and check my desk for more hidden cameras. Finn's response comes a minute after my question, as though he's taking longer to process things.

"No, thanks, Brook. I had some yogurt today." I pause.

"When did you have that?"

"Around ten." I glance at the clock on the stove. It's three in the afternoon. I throw some chicken in a pan with olive oil, basil, parsley, and other spices that I find in the cabinet. Once it's cooked, I take a smaller piece, put it on a plate, take a fork out of the drawer, fill up a glass of water, and bring everything to Finn. He looks at me as I come in with a soft smile on my face.

"You need to eat, Finn," I tell him gently, putting the plate down on Drew's desk in front of him. He glances at the food like an uninterested cat. "Starving yourself isn't healthy."

"I'm not starving myself."

"Did you go to the gym today?" Another pause. Finn continues to stare at the chicken that's getting colder by the second.

"No."

"Oh, Finn," I pity, letting the conversation dissolve into silence. "Have you been here all day?" He nods. "Did you go to class?" He shakes his head.

"Didn't feel like it," he says quietly, picking up the fork and poking at the chicken, which is cooked so well that it falls apart on impact. "Are you close to finding him? The kidnapper?"

"Yeah. Close. I just need to tie up a few loose ends." I offer him a smile, and he accepts it weakly, turning back to the chicken and putting some in his mouth. I've never seen him this quiet or scared, but I relate to the feeling of wanting to disappear inside of oneself until this is all over.

I quickly shove some chicken in my mouth and change into something a bit more intimidating than Nate's sweatshirt and leggings. After throwing on Drew's leather jacket over a tight-fitting maroon t-shirt and lacing up my combat boots, I snatch my purse from its hook behind the door and leave the apartment.

The cold air plays with my hair as I wait for a bus that'll take me downtown. From there, I'll connect to a bus that'll bring me to the outskirts of Northwich, where I'll disembark. On both buses I ride, the passengers are less than favorable. There's a man with eyes that won't stop darting around, a woman humming to herself, and a child who can't be more than twelve but seems to have no parents in sight. I try to keep to myself in the back of the bus, my headphones in my ears. As always, the feeling of being watched follows me like a shadow.

By the time I get off my second bus, it's almost four. I've been dropped off on what seems to be a random corner outside of the main city. There's litter everywhere, no sidewalks, and tons of inexpensive beaten down cars driving around. My attention isn't on the cars so much as it is on the huge brick building to my left.

Like the SHA house, the brick building has an ominous energy to it. The sides of building are mostly covered with little slat windows chiseled into them. Outside is a concrete courtyard with chain-linked fencing around it and barbed wire on top of that. In fact, the fence goes around the entire facility. There are tall imposing guard towers, with armed men peering out of the tops. Even though it's a small facility, it's armed like Guantanamo Bay. Just looking at the place scares the hell out of me.

And why shouldn't it? I'm looking at a prison.

I walk up to the main entrance of the building and a guard at the desk inside buzzes me in. As I approach him, he stares me down, wondering what a 19-year-old girl could possibly want here. He appears to be in his late 40s, with a full head of hair and piercing eyes.

"Can I help you?" His voice is gravelly and low. I involuntarily gulp before speaking.

"I'm here to visit an inmate," I plainly state, mustering up the strength to push past my fear.

"Visiting hours are almost over," says the guard in a disaffected voice.

"It's for a story for WRDW News." The guard looks up at me and raises his eyebrows, unimpressed. That's when I suddenly wonder if I'm the first person from the college to show up unannounced.

"What's your name?"

"Brooklyn Perce."

"Identification." I pull out my wallet and give him my license. He looks between me and my license a few times before handing it back to me, together with a form. "Fill this out." I take a pen from the counter and quickly scribble in my information. When I give it back to him, he looks it over and asks, "Who do you want to see?"

"Taylor King." The guard types in something on his computer. He slides me another side eye.

"You're not on his visitation list. Is he expecting you?"

"No." When I see he's considering turning me away, I pipe up again. "It'll only take ten minutes. Fifteen tops." The guard looks at me and sighs, clearly just wanting me to go away as soon as possible.

"Alright." He gets up out of his chair, and he's surprisingly shorter than I thought he was. The guard leads me down the hallway and through a set of iron bar doors that have to be opened with the passkey on his belt. There are guards every thirty feet, along the hallway, which makes me feel safe and terrified at the same time. I can see the guard is leading me to the end of the hallway, which has a big metal door. There's a guard in front of that too.

"Who's she?" he asks in a gruff voice.

"Wants to see Inmate 0115," says the desk guy. The guard looks at me.

"Who're you?"

"Brooklyn Perce. I went to school with him. I'm doing a follow-up story about his incident from last year." When I give my situation one more second of thought, I figure I probably shouldn't be lying to these men, who both look like they can break my neck in two seconds. The two men exchange looks. Finally, the guard caves.

"Alright, put her in the first room. I'll go get him." *For a place holding an attempted murderer, they're very lax here.* The guard swipes his pass to the door and punches in a code on the keypad to the right. I hear deadbolts unlock, and the guard goes in, shutting the door behind him.

The guy behind the desk shows me into a bare room, with one window on the opposite wall and a mirror on the wall with the door. I'm assuming it's a two-way mirror, judging by the windows into other rooms I saw while walking down the hallway. There's one metal table in the center of the room, with two chairs on either side of it. The tabletop has a metal loop welded to it. I go to sit in a chair, but the man stops me.

"Put your hands up like this," he says, putting his arms in a surrender position. I do as he asks, and he pats me down to make sure I have nothing on me. He empties my purse on the table and looks through all the junk I have in there. When he determines I'm not there to break Taylor out, he nods. "Sit. He'll be in soon." I repack my things and sit down. The man shuts the door on his way out, and I'm alone, left to consider my decisions.

I told Ryker I would only do this if I was desperate. My boyfriend is gone, and so is my roommate. That would qualify as desperation. Mask Man has left me no leads so far, and he's clearly trying to be a copycat of Taylor. I figured I should consult him. A little laugh escapes me as I think how happy he'll be to know his work is being continued, even in his absence.

I bounce my leg up and down in anticipation, which makes a little welcomed squeaking sound. It's so quiet in this room that, if I sat in here alone for too long, I'd surely start to hallucinate sounds to keep me company. Thankfully, someone opens the door.

In skulks Taylor King, in all his decrepit glory. His muddy brown hair is greasy, his build has gone from healthy to bony, and his grey eyes look beadier, sunken back into his skull, like a gruesome Halloween decoration. The sickly green jumpsuit color does nothing for him, although I don't think it would for anyone. He sits down in the chair across from me and glares at me through his long, stringy hair. My heart feels like it's going to leap out of my chest. I feel queasy, but I stop myself from throwing up. My nightmares have done nothing to prepare me for seeing him in person. The sound of the guard hooking Taylor's handcuffs through the loop in the table brings me back to the moment. Taylor's ankle chains are attached to the legs of the chair, and the guard yanks on them to make sure they're secure.

Good. He can't reach out and strangle me from across the table.

"Fifteen minutes," says the guard to me before leaving us alone. The door shuts with a resonating *BANG.* Taylor and I just stare at each other, his eyes trying to pierce holes through my head. I can hear my pounding heart. I can't bring myself to talk. Seeing this human makes me want to run and hide. The look on his face indicates he's fantasizing about breaking his chains, jumping over the table, and killing me. *Why the hell did I come here again?*

"Look who's here," Taylor finally says in a jarringly calm voice that sends chills up my arms. He chuckles. "When they told me it was you, I knew it was going to be good." I swallow and say nothing. Taylor dons a cocky smile. "There's no way you'd come here unless you were desperate." He gives me a once over and clicks his tongue disapprovingly. "And, Perce, you look *desperate.*" Taylor folds his hands on the table, the handcuffs clinking ominously. He settles into his chair with such confidence that my skin erupts with goosebumps. "So, what is it?"

"Someone is kidnapping students from campus. I think you're behind it," I accuse him in a flat tone. Taylor raises an eyebrow while keeping the same neutral expression.

"Really? Interesting," he says as though this isn't news to him at all. "You're so stupid, Perce. Thinking I'd help you." I swallow hard, and he leans in. The lighting makes his face look hollower. "You're selfish.

You wouldn't be here unless the kidnappings directly affected you." Judging by the way he looks at me, my facial expression must have changed. Taylor's smile grows wider. "But they have." My stomach hurts more. "Who'd they take, Brooklyn? Was it that artist charity case of yours? What's her name?" Taylor pauses like he's pretending to think. "Oh. *Drew*."

"How'd you—?"

"Would've been fun to watch that. I bet she put up a fight," Taylor says as though he's reminiscing.

"How'd you know about her?" I press.

"She's obvious. She's like your pathetic little sister that you feel the need to protect. But she's gotten herself into more shit than you have. She can take care of herself, I'm sure." Taylor leans in and searches my eyes. My leg bounces underneath the table and my palms are sweating. I try to hold back a shudder as I feel his gaze permeate my soul. "But there's someone else, isn't there?" I say nothing as Taylor glares at me like a predator, wracking his brain and finally coming up with another person. "Did they take Nathan?" Taylor whispers, a crazed, gleeful look in his eyes. When I purse my lips, Taylor does a guttural chuckle. "Your trophy boyfriend, Nathan Stevenson, is *gone*?" I breathe out measuredly through my nose as Taylor's bizarre expression solidifies. "Oh, you poor bitch. You must be going insane without him, you codependent, clingy brat."

"Shut the fuck up," I snarl. Taylor laughs.

"Oh, she still has her bite!" He bites his teeth at me like a dog. I flinch, and he smiles again. "And there it is. She's here because her boyfriend is going to die. Wish I was out there so I could help torture the hell out of him."

"I wish I'd killed you," I hiss through my teeth, my fingernails digging into my palms.

181

"Oh, you don't mean that," he says with a pout. "But wouldn't life have been so much easier for you, though, if you did? You would've rid the world of me, would've had all the fame you crave, and yet, here I am."

"I don't want fame."

"Bullshit," Taylor hisses. "Why do people do anything? They want to be recognized. Your *brilliant* mind might not get that yet, but it will. All you want is to seem legitimate to keep your boyfriends happy. And they keep you around for their own selfish reasons. Stevenson's a prick, but he's not dumb. If you're important, he knows he is too. And Ryker Williams, he keeps you around for the *thrill.*" Taylor scoffs as though the mention of Ryker's name brings a bad taste to his mouth. "You make that asshole feel like he's some redeemed hero."

"He's not an asshole," I retort. Taylor raises his eyebrow, clearly taken aback.

"Well, look at that." He grins at me. "You've finally given into him, now that Nathan is gone?"

"No!"

"Liar. I wouldn't be surprised if Williams captured Nathan. He always said he wanted Nathan out of the way. He wanted to kill your boyfriend. Did he tell you that?" For once, I have nothing to say. Taylor laughs again through his bared teeth. "Left out that little gem, did he? Gave you his little sob story about how he was the *only one* in the fraternity who wanted to *save* you!" He says this in a high, mocking tone, infuriating me even more. "He's a liar like you, like me."

"We are *not* the same."

"You keep on thinking that."

"You miserable, evil piece of shit," I finally manage to say. "I will *never* be like you."

"Never? That's a strong word. *Never* be like me." Taylor appears as though he's musing over the word. "You just haven't been pushed hard enough, Perce. You haven't found your limit. You might think you have, but the worst is yet to come." I swallow the bile rising in my throat.

"I'm not here for your games." Taylor chuckles to himself, a sound I choose to ignore. "You clearly know something about the kidnappings. How would you know about Nate and Drew if you didn't?"

"Touchy, touchy," clicks Taylor disapprovingly. "So easy to rouse, Miss Perce. Might want to think about controlling that."

"Answer the goddamn question," I growl.

"Even if I knew something, would I tell you? You're smarter than that, so I thought." At the annoyed twitch of my nose, Taylor smiles triumphantly. "I wish I did know something, though. I would help them. I would love the chance to make you miserable again."

"You don't have any friends or any siblings at Resslar?"

"Luckily for you, I'm technically an only child. My sibling would be more fucked up than I am." My eyebrows crease at his little smirk.

"'Technically'? What does 'technically' mean?"

"Let's not get into my sordid family history, Perce. We both have daddy issues, best to leave it at that." For the first time since knowing him, I see a flicker of disappointment on his face. He composes himself quickly. "And I wouldn't call them friends so much as puppets."

"What are you talking about?"

"People I can manipulate. Like you do with Williams when you string him along." I try to keep my temper under control, but I remember how Gavin described Jordyn's many male friends as 'collectables.' My stomach hurts even more.

"Any girlfriends? Exes maybe?" Taylor raises an eyebrow before continuing.

"Funny you ask. I had a girlfriend once. Crazy bitch, even for me. We broke up long before I got my hands on you, though." I nod. Taylor tilts his head a bit, knowing I'm mulling something else over. He groans under his breath. "That all, Perce?"

"No." I gulp. "When I visited Ryker to ask about the fraternity, he said if you had killed me, you were going to leave me in the house to rot ..." Taylor's mouth twists into that horrible grin again.

"Mm. I wanted nothing to do with you after I would've killed you. Tossing you in the basement and letting you fall apart was what we'd agreed on, but your boyfriend, Williams, wanted to bury you in the cemetery. Stupid idea. Your body could be easily traced back to us." He licks his bottom lip and glances over my upper body. It makes me squirm where I sit. "But once I get out and hunt you down, I'll bury you half dead in the cemetery. It's a great place to hide things you want to get rid of." I lean in and put my forearms on the table, staring into his eyes. Taylor's left eyebrow is slightly raised in a devious smile when he copies my movements. "And I know the people who hide things there won't be as forgiving with their captured bodies as Williams was with yours." His words freeze me to the core, but I'm trying to memorize as much as I can.

Mask Man might be hiding something in the cemetery.

Mask Man is going to kill everyone he's captured.

"That's fifteen," says the guard, entering the room and making me jump. Taylor, on the other hand, doesn't flinch when the door opens. As the man undoes the chains, Taylor only stares at me like a hyena who got screwed out of its prey by a lion. Taylor stands as the guard relocks his handcuffs and takes his place behind the prisoner. I watch him leave as he says his one last wish.

"Good luck, Brooklyn. I hope you die."

18

When I get home from the prison, I immediately go into Kenni's room to see if she's there. Thankfully, she's sitting on her bed doing homework. She looks up as I enter.

"Hey, where were you?" she asks as I take a seat at her desk.

"Prison, where they're keeping Taylor." Her jaw drops, and she stops writing, her pen making a stray mark on the paper.

"Okay, I have *so* many questions, the first being how did they let you *in* there? They knew you were the one who *put him in there*, right?" she incredulously replies.

"I don't think so. Taylor looks awful."

"Well, I'm not surprised. Wasn't that good-looking to begin with."

"Did Finn go home?"

"Yeah, an hour ago. He said he might come back, but I think sitting in Drew's room is just making him worse. Getting back to the more pressing issue of why the hell did you go to the prison?"

"I thought Taylor would know something about the kidnappings, and it turns out, even when he's not on campus, he's on campus. It's terrifying."

"So, he knows the guy who's after you?"

"I think so. How's that possible, though? He said he didn't have any siblings or friends, just an ex." I reconsider. "Well, he said he *technically* doesn't have any siblings." Kenni raises a skeptical eyebrow.

"And what does that mean?"

"Beats me."

"He could just be lying."

"Yeah, he's good at that." I take another second or two to think. "There's something that keeps bothering me, though. If they want to kill me, they know where I live and when I'm home, so why don't they just come here and finish it? I'd prefer that to them stalking me."

"Are you *critiquing* their stalking methods?" Kenni snickers. When she puts it like that, I laugh. "Look, half of the fun for these sorts of people is the game. I'm sure Mask Man is getting off on the idea of stringing you along until he finally decides to get you."

"You're probably right." I go into my room and drop onto my bed. When I look over at my desk, there's nothing there, besides Jared's crucifix necklace. I still don't know what the NEXT TO note means. Next to what? Taylor's clue was clear to me. The graveyard holds something, and if I don't get there soon, people I love are going to die. Or maybe they're already dead.

Ryker wanted to bury me in the cemetery. I think of the towering mausoleums covered in ivy and vines. There's nothing inside most of them since all their inhabitants died and decayed decades ago. That's probably the case with most of the coffins too. I wonder if there was anyone buried inside of the church I explored. There can't be anyone in there, though. The gangs have taken it over and would've surely sniffed out the bodies. Hell, they graffitied over the crucifix and made Jesus cry blood—

Wait.

I spring up from my bed and snatch Jared's crucifix from my desk. An image flashes in my mind, of the abandoned church and the massive statue of Jesus on the floor with red spray paint seeping out of His eyes. Suddenly, it all makes sense, and I chide myself for being so stupid.

Next to the church in the graveyard where Ryker wanted to bury me.

I quickly throw on Drew's leather jacket and my black Doc Martens, jamming the boots onto my feet as I run through my apartment. Kenni emerges from her room in confusion and watches me frantically run around.

"What are you—?"

"Kenni, I'm going to the graveyard. If I'm not back in two hours, call the police! Tell 'em the abandoned church in the back!" I call as I reluctantly stop at the front door to put my shoes on properly, so as not to twist my ankle. Kenni quickly swings into the living room.

"You're not going alone!"

"Oh, yes, I am. They want me, not you." Kenni seems at a loss for words. Before I start toward the door, I go into the kitchen and grab a small paring knife from the drawer, stuffing it into my jeans. Kenni is looking at me like I've lost it. "Call the police. That's your job, alright?"

"Shouldn't you tell Greenwood—?"

"GOD, Ken, this is a matter of life and death. I'll be damned if I wait for that asshole's approval. Call the cops if I'm not back in two hours."

"Brook—!" I slam the door on her calling my name. There's ice in the air that has already begun freezing the little hairs on my face. I try to fight the cold as I run past the bus stop, to the entrance of West Campus, all the way to the main road, where I finally encounter traffic. People honk their horns at me as I sprint across the street. I'm ready to run into the graveyard, but when I get to where the grass meets the sidewalk, I pause. It looks so ominous this time of night. There's even a little fog covering the ground, blurring the snow that's sitting on the headstones. I consider calling the police –like my father, my mother, and the cops want me to do –and heading back home. But for all I know, Nate, Drew, and the others are locked up somewhere here, probably wounded and starving and alone. They can't afford another second out here. After taking a deep breath, I venture into the darkness.

Every few feet, I look over my shoulder. It gets colder as I travel to the back of the place, and once I get down the huge hill, the fog is up to my knees. The graveyard is a maze, and the weather makes it even more disorienting. It's so quiet and still that it's unsettling. I can't be sure where I came from or where I've been. I've probably gone in a few circles. Maybe I should've brought Kenni with me. It would've been nice to have some company, but I don't want her to get hurt. Mask Man only wants me anyway.

I feel like I've been down this gravel path before. The names on the headstones start to sound familiar. *Young, Freedman, Livingston.* I'm so wrapped up in reading the names to steady my mind that I trip on a rock and tumble down another hill. Once I reach the bottom and stop rolling, I feel bruises forming all along my right arm and leg. I groan in pain as I get to my feet and dust myself off, a groan of pain escapes me. When I look around, I realize where I am. The steeples of the two churches rise high above the fog, one of them half collapsed, the other proudly towering over its building. I gulp as I slowly walk towards the decrepit church. *Next to, next to, next to.*

My feet feel heavy, but I have to keep walking-

No, you can go home.

They're out here alone-

You know where they are. You can call the police.

They're my friends and they need me-

You could die.

I don't care-

Crunch.

I spin around as fast as possible to see what's behind me. I think I see a shadow quickly flit out of sight. Cautiously, I keep walking, rounding the side of the church near the train tracks, keeping my eyes on the ground. My heart is beating fast, and I'm hyper-aware of everything going on around me. I'm shaking but not because of the cold. In fact, I hardly notice the temperature anymore.

You need to leave. Get out of here before you get hurt.

It's okay. It'll be okay-

Brooklyn, you need to leave.

Not now, I'm so close-

Crunch.

I whirl around again. The fingers I have clenched around the little knife in my belt have gone numb. My breath meets the air in a white cloud as I search the pitch darkness around me. When I turn around, my head is on a swivel, and thank God it is because I almost stepped in a hole.

A person-sized hole.

When I shine my phone's flashlight into the pit, I realize it's about five feet deep and six feet long. It's dug crudely, and the shovel is laying at its side. At the other end of the ditch is a headstone. With a gulp, I point my flashlight at it, and my breath hitches in my throat.

The word *Perce* has been carved into a slab of stone that's standing upright. *There is absolutely no way this is real.* I squeeze my eyes shut, but when I reopen them, the headstone's still there. A soft whimper escapes my lips.

CRUNCH.

I turn away from my grave and walk forward a few feet.

"Who's there?" I call to the darkness, putting my flashlight away and gripping the knife harder. "Come out." As I keep inching forward, a human shadow appears in front of me. The silhouette doesn't look upright. By my estimate, it should be a little over six feet, but it's hunched over. When I get closer, I can see the familiar brown hair of my boyfriend. It's Nate. I let out a relieved laugh, but as I walk, I realize that was premature.

Nate looks like he's lost a match with an MMA fighter. There are bruises on his jaw and around his right eye. On his chin and coming out of his mouth, I see dried blood. The gash in his leg runs the length of his thigh, which explains why he's favoring one leg over another. His clothes are torn like a rabid dog got to him. He looks tired, but I couldn't be happier to see him alive.

"Nate!" I exclaim in relief. Once I take the first couple of steps toward him, a hand closes around my wrist and firmly holds me in place.

Almost as if in slow motion, I pivot around, and come face-to-face with Mask Man.

"NATE!" I shriek, my head whipping back to my boyfriend. Mask Man starts to drag me backwards, so I turn, trying to hit him. He punches me in the face, grabs my other wrist, and twists it past its capability, which elicits a scream from me. I see Nate trying to run to my aid, but something pulls him backward into the fog.

"BROOKLYN!" roars Nate as he tries to release himself. Mask Man's foot kicks me in the stomach, and I go limp as the air is taken from my lungs. I try to punch him, but he's already tied my wrists with some rough cable. My blood pounds in my ears as Mask Man pulls me towards the grave marked with my name. As much as I try to dig my heels into the ground, they slip on the ice and can't break the frozen soil. With a final push, I'm shoved backwards into the pit.

I fall five feet.

My skull cracks on something hard.

I pass out.

19

There's a throbbing pain in my head as I slowly open my eyes to take in the surrounding horror movie.

My wrists and ankles are bound to the arms and legs of the chair I'm sitting in. The blood coming from my nose is drying on my lips and chin. My limbs ache as though I've been used as a punching bag. I'm shaking from the cold and shock. Once my heart begins to race, my eyes dart around the room as I try to figure out where I am.

The room looks like a small cavern. It's freezing in here. I can see my breath as I huff in and out. The walls look wet, and there are little icicles forming on the ceiling. The drips from the icicles softly plop on the floor. It looks like catacombs were built underneath the church, but everything has rotted. The smell of decaying wood and bodies assaults my nose, making me feel nauseated.

Mask Man is sitting across from me, snickering. The back of the chair he's sitting in is facing me as his legs straddle it. His long arms are folded over one another on the back, and he's leaning forward as though peering at a zoo animal. My heart pounds faster when he stops laughing and just stares at my face like he's in a trance, waiting for me to say something.

"Nice place," I say sarcastically, trying to hide the tremor in my voice. "Really nailed the ambiance."

"You're scared," he says in an odd robotic voice. I say nothing and steel my face. "You pretend to be strong, but you're a scared little girl." There's a pause as I dig my fingernails into my palms. Mask Man tilts his head to the side. I try to see through the eye holes in the mask, but he's too far away. "I would've expected you to plead for your life," he adds.

"I'm not about the theatrics," I snarl. "The second time you get kidnapped, you're not as scared." Mask Man chuckles again.

"But you are." He stands, and I try not to shrink back into my chair when I see his imposing height. Now I can see a sheath dangling at his side from his belt. A glint of silver flashes at me. *There's no way.* "I've seen you in your nightmares, Brooklyn. You're positively terrified." My upper lip starts twitching in contempt. "You pretend not to be scared out of your mind, but I can see through it. You can't hide anything from me. I know you're afraid." He smirks as I sit there in silence. Mask Man steps closer until he's about six feet away from where I sit. "But I don't care. In fact, I prefer you this way."

"Glad I can amuse you," I spit. Mask Man laughs. I breathe harder through my nose as he comes within a foot of me. The feeling I got in Fraanco is back. If I weren't tied to the chair, I'd be running, scouring every inch of the walls for some exit. Mask Man's presence is making my skin crawl.

"You have some nerve joking. I can see you shiver from here."

"You have good eyes then. Wish I could see them." When he doesn't talk, I keep going. "C'mon, you're not going to let me die without seeing *you*, the person who's been making my life a living hell. I feel like I'm owed that much." He just stares at me, and I press on. "So, who are you? And why do you want me dead?" Mask Man considers me for a moment, then slowly lifts his gloved hands and removes the hood from his head. With one motion, he takes off the mask and shakes his hair out. The mask drops from his hand to the floor. When I look into his eyes for the first time, I realize I've seen then before.

It's Gavin.

"*You*?" I whisper. Gavin smirks as his grey eyes survey the horror on my face.

"Gotcha," he says. I'm stunned. Gavin puts his hands on my thighs and leans in, his nose five inches from mine. My breathing can't establish a regular pattern as he gazes at me, grinning like a jackal. "Aw, you poor thing. Stunned into silence."

"This isn't happening. This isn't real," I say to myself as I search his eyes for any sign that this is just another nightmare.

"Oh, but it is," Gavin says, the echo in the room dragging out the 's'. "I'm the one who's been driving you insane. I took your roommate and your boyfriend from you. I snuck into your apartment and delivered those little clues to drag out your misery." My lips become a thin line as I stare at Gavin who couldn't be happier.

"Get away from me," I hiss through my teeth. Gavin's smile reminds me of Taylor's grin when he'd realized that Ryker was in love with me.

"This was so fun, Brooklyn. I thought this would be harder, but you're so *easy* to manipulate. Once you find a story, you become invested in figuring it out. It almost makes me want to admire you," Gavin says, with his lips inches from my face.

"What have I ever done to you?" I whisper. The freshman laughs and finally backs away, turning and pacing a few steps towards the wall.

"What did you *do* to me?" he repeats. Gavin turns around and grits his teeth. "You put my brother in jail. You destroyed him. You broke my family when it was already shattered to begin with. For that, you deserve what you have coming."

"Your brother ..." Then it clicks.

Luckily for you, I'm technically an only child.

"Taylor's your *brother*?" I say in disbelief.

"Surprise," Gavin says with a chuckle, one eyebrow perfectly arched upward. He walks back towards me as I try to piece together the puzzle.

"But your last name is—"

"Wryte. I took my mother's last name. Taylor took our father's. It's the only way I could've gotten into this school."

"Taylor said he was an only child," I tell him, though I remember the irritated way his nose twitched when I asked him.

"He said that?" Gavin scoffs. "Figures. He likes to pretend I don't exist, that I'm not related to him. He thinks I'm weak. I'm not. And to prove it, I'm gonna finally finish what he started." My stomach twists as I remember what Taylor said about his would-be brother: *He'd be more fucked up than Taylor.* To stall my death, I keep talking.

"You want to earn Taylor's respect? You can't. No matter what you do, he still won't call you his brother. You're stupid to think otherwise."

"You don't know *anything* about him," Gavin fumes through his teeth.

"I know he's a murderous, manipulative son of a bitch." At that, Gavin whips out a sword he has in his belt and points it at me. I'm taken aback by the weapon, so I flinch into the back of the chair.

"Don't you *ever* say that about my brother," Gavin threatens.

"Where'd you get that from?" I breathe in horror, looking at the rusted blade.

"You can find a lot of things on the internet if you just look. Like how your boyfriend found one of these by digging through a basement." He admires the thing in his hand.

"Little much, don't you think?" I say.

"An eye for an eye. I roughed up the blade a bit. I want it to hurt when it goes through you," replies Gavin. Despite the sword in front of me, something tells me he's never swung it in his life. This gives me enough confidence to call his bluff.

"So, you're gonna kill me?" I ask, a little smirk on my face. I sit up straighter in the chair. "Alright. Go on. Do it." Gavin looks at my smug face and makes his upper lip stiff as he tries to muster the courage to follow through with his vendetta. "C'mon, Gavin. Kill me." There's a flicker in his eye, something slight, but I see it. Something is stopping him from doing it. I'm staring him down to see if he waivers again, but he won't budge.

"The fun's starting without me, eh?" I jump as I hear another augmented voice. Gavin and I turn to a door on my left. There's a dropping sensation in my stomach when I see another man in a mask enter. Gavin has the sly smile of a fox. I shrink into my chair. The new Mask Man is also wearing all black and doesn't look away from my terrified face, as he walks towards Gavin. "Look who finally figured it out."

"You're late," Gavin chides, putting the sword back in its sheath.

"Stevenson put up a fight, but she got him down." *She?* The pit in my stomach grows as the new Mask Man stops right in front of me. "Hey there, gorgeous." He cocks his head to the left and slowly kneels in front of me. The man slowly takes his mask off as he stares me down. My entire body goes numb when I see the smirking face of my trainee, Conor. His grin grows when he sees the horror on my face. "Having a nice night?"

"I should've known it was you," I say through my teeth.

"You really should've." His eyes scan my body, lingering on the wounds I've been given by his boss. Conor puts his hands on the arms of my chair and slowly gets up so his head hangs over me. He chuckles. The longer he stares at me, the dirtier I feel, and the more goosebumps erupt on my arms. "Torture suits you."

"Calm down, Conor," orders Gavin. Conor rounds on him, his mood shifting on a dime.

"Don't you tell me to calm down, Wryte. This bitch has treated me like shit, and I've put up with it because of *you* and your stupid plan—"

"Yeah? And who wanted to be a part of that plan, Valree?" The men glare at each other. Gavin steps forward threateningly. "You lay a hand on her, I kill you." Conor stares Gavin in the eyes, then walks back

198

over to me and punches me across the face. Tears involuntarily stream down my eyes as I try to blink away the spots of light in my vision. As much as Gavin sounded like he meant his threat to Conor, a little smile can't help but pass over his face. He loves seeing me in pain, just like his brother. Conor grabs the hair on the top of my head, forces it backwards, and puts his lips inches from mine.

"Scream," he softly demands.

"Go fuck yourself," I say with clenched teeth. Conor punches me again with the opposite hand, and this time, I feel something metal underneath the glove he's wearing.

"Scream!" he presses.

"Shut up!" I shriek. That gets me another hit to the cheek.

"Enough!" Gavin roars. Conor obeys this time. Breathing heavily through his nose, Conor slowly lets go of me and walks back to his partner. They hold eye contact the entire time.

"She's been a nosey and condescending bitch, and you expect me to let her sit there, knowing that no matter what I do, she can't fight back?" Conor spits through his teeth.

"Yes." Gavin says calmly and walks back towards me, leaving Conor standing there, fuming. As he glances down at me, the blood coming from my nose thickens, and the bruise by my eye shows its colors. He takes the ends of my hair and twirls them around his finger, his beady eyes searching my face. "Because if you give this one a chance, she'll fight back like she did with my brother. And knowing you, Valree, your wanting to pin her to a wall will get the better of you, and I can't have that."

"You're just like your brother," I mutter. Gavin's eyes light up.

"Yeah?" he asks.

"Yeah, he liked monologuing too." For that, I get punched in the stomach. My back slams into the chair, and I cough violently, flecks of blood staining my pants as I do. Gavin turns around and looks towards the door. He looks at Conor.

"Where is she?" he asks his crony. From somewhere, I hear the muffled yells of my boyfriend. I bolt upright in the chair, temporarily forgetting my pain, and turn towards the direction the sound is coming from. The screams die down, and from behind a door comes Jordyn wearing a black ensemble that's gleaming with a deep red sheen. Gavin's sneaky smile returns.

"Speak of the devil," he says with a predatorial snarl. Jordyn walks in with her hands clasped behind her back and head held high.

"He's down. No thanks to you," Jordyn says, glaring at Conor. He doesn't say anything, which I assume is due to Gavin's presence.

"Excellent." Gavin's voice makes my skin crawl.

"What did you do to him?" I ask, my tongue tasting a bit of blood as I open my mouth. Jordyn doesn't seem to notice my question. She saunters over to Gavin whose arm makes its way across her tightly bound waist. Conor's nose begins to subtly jerk in annoyance as he looks at them.

"What *did* you do to him?" Gavin asks again in a silky voice. Jordyn just looks at me and lets out a girly giggle that further ignites my hatred. My fingernails are digging into my palms, adding to my physical pain.

"Hello, Brooklyn! So glad you could join us," she purrs. My upper lip starts to twitch.

"Where's Nate?" I growl in a register I've never heard myself use. Jordyn untangles herself from Gavin.

"He's fine, hon," she replies, in what she must think is a reassuring tone. "Why would you think I'd want to hurt him?" After staring daggers at her for about a second, she starts giggling like a lunatic. Gavin looks like he couldn't be more in love. Conor has almost finished blending into the wall behind him. As I stare at her with loathing, I realize something.

"You're Taylor's ex, aren't you?" At the mention of his name, she stops laughing. Gavin looks less than thrilled that I know this information. "How was dating him?" I sarcastically ask. "He told me you were nuts."

"He said that?" Jordyn says, putting a hand to her heart. "I'm touched."

"Of course, you are," Conor finally groans, still sulking in the corner, with his eyes fixated on me. It's quiet as I look at the three of them. They know what they're doing, and they're fine with it. Hell, one of them even has a *sword* to intimidate me, in a true act of commitment to the crime. Taylor was right. They *are* crazier than him. Sure, he was unhinged, but young and reckless kids out for vengeance are arguably worse. Jordyn turns back to Gavin.

"I'm bored. When do we kill her?" she whines like a child. After I decide I can no longer contain myself, I burst out laughing, and all three of them turn to me. Gavin looks at me like I'm scum on his shoe.

"You're not gonna kill me!" I snicker, nodding to Gavin. "His brother was too scared to. What makes you think he's going to?"

"He's better than his brother," Jordyn defends, walking away from him and towards me. "Gavin's crueler than Taylor could've ever—"

"Really, so why am I still alive?" I fire at her. That shuts her up. The smug look on her face slips as I grin through the blood coming out of my mouth. "If you're gonna kill me, just do it. I'll be happy to end this nightmare. I'll be even happier knowing where I am is nowhere near where you will be. Sure, I'll die, but you won't ever be able to touch me ever again. So do me a favor and just let it be over."

Jordyn's nose twitches in disdain. Conor looks like he wants to attack me. Every muscle in Gavin's body is tight with anger.

The room is silent.

Then, Gavin stalks over to me and seizes me by the throat. My body immediately tenses up as he starts to squeeze, the veins in his forehead popping and the whites of his eyes glowing. My mouth opens and closes like a fish as I start to gasp for air. Jordyn and Conor make no move to stop him as he puts my neck in a tightening vice.

"Don't you *ever* talk to her like that again," threatens Gavin, throwing my neck backwards so my head hits the chair. Even though my skull hurts, I savor the cool air flowing into my lungs. When he lets go of my throat, he walks backwards, looking at me the entire time like a hawk stalking a mouse.

"Where is he?" I croak in a ragged voice, as I watch Jordyn clutch Gavin like a child with a toy. "Where's Nate?" Conor laughs at me from the corner, finally coming back into the light.

"I'm so glad I was the one who suggested taking him from you." At my look of contempt, Connor broadly smiles. "One of my better ideas."

"Let me see him," I demand. Gavin's face is stony. "Take me to him." Conor looks to Gavin for approval. Gavin carefully draws out his sword and nods to Conor and Jordyn. They take the cuffs off my wrists and ankles but keep a firm grip on me.

"One wrong move," Gavin threatens quietly. Conor wrestles my wrists to my back and cuffs them again to keep me on a leash. Gavin walks backwards in front of me, with the tip of the sword pointed at my chest, as they lead me to the door that Jordyn entered from. Conor still has a firm grip on my chain which only gets tighter as we enter the new room.

This space is round like the first room and has a partially blocked sewer grate on the ceiling, which lets in a small amount of dim light. Somehow, it's colder in here than it was in the other room. There's snow on the ground, and massive icicles latch themselves onto the stone walls. Underneath some of them are bodies slumped down on the dirt.

There are five of them evenly spaced around the room. They're all attached to the wall in one way or another. I first recognize the red hair of Issac, who is the furthest from me and looks asleep. His head is back against the wall, and his skin catches the light. I can see he has black eyes. Looking to the left, I see Jared, who is on the floor, with his clothes shredded to bits. I can only imagine what his skin looks like underneath. On the other side of Issac is Nicole, who doesn't appear to be breathing and is curled up in a ball on the grimy floor. Drew looks like she's still alive since her eyes widen when she sees me. Her eager screams are muffled by the gag in her mouth. Drew looks over to her right, and there he is.

My boyfriend.

Nate looks like he's been beaten more than the rest. He has something in his mouth too, but it looks like he's chewed on it. When he sees me, he tries to yell something too. My heart immediately sinks, seeing how haggard he looks. Though I wasn't the one who kidnapped him, I can't help but feel entirely responsible for his beaten appearance.

"Nate!" I yell happily. I try to run to him, but I'm snatched backwards by the chain that Conor is still holding. Gavin laughs at me and comes in between me and Nate. He's still holding the sword.

"Where do you think you're going?" he asks cockily, pointing the blade at me.

"You have me, let them go," I say desperately, dropping the act from earlier. "*Please.* You've tortured them enough. Let them go." Gavin clucks his tongue.

"Now, that's not the Brooklyn I know from those stories. The Brooklyn I heard about never begged or pleaded. She *bravely* defeated her kidnappers in a *daring* escape attempt." I feel like spitting at his feet as he talks to me in a patronizing tone. "She fought *heroically* to save her own skin from the *terrifying* men." The chains on my wrists loosen and then come off, dropping to the floor with a clatter. Still, I make no sudden movements as the tip of the sword is about a foot away from driving into my ribcage. "So that's what she's going to do." When I glance behind me, Jordyn and Conor have smaller swords pointed at my back. I'm surrounded. Suppressing a bark of laughter, I meet Gavin's self-righteous smile.

"Alright, then."

20

Unsurprisingly, Jordyn starts the games off with a weak jab that I easily avoid by ducking. My next move is sweeping my leg underneath her feet, knocking her off balance. The heeled boots she's wearing don't help things. As her head hits the ground, her sword goes skittering away from her. I try to lunge for it, but I feel the tip of another blade poke at my back. When I turn, it's Conor.

"Shit," I swear. I get up and run straight towards him, taking him by surprise. My foot makes contact with his stomach, and I send him flying backwards. His body almost hits Drew who surveys his unconscious body with huge eyes. Though I'm proud of my strength, I'm not allowed a second of awe because Jordyn has made it back to her feet.

"C'mon, you look like an idiot," I tell her with a mocking expression. Jordyn makes a sound of annoyance and comes at me head-on with the blade, like I wanted her to. I side-step the sword and punch Jordyn square in the face as she runs past me. Jordyn screams and falls to the ground immediately, cracking her head on the way down. The sound her head makes when it hits the ground is something out of a slasher movie. I dive for her sword and quickly grab it, getting back to my feet and facing Gavin. My chest is heaving up and down, my body is coursing with adrenaline, and my eyes are wide, as I get ready to strike. All my senses and emotions are heightened, my eyesight, my hearing, my fear. Slightly alarmed, Gavin looks at me as my body vibrates in waiting for him to lash out.

"Thought you'd be at least breaking a sweat from fighting them," he says.

"You wanted to tire me out. It worked," I say, following his movements. Gavin chuckles, like I've caught him red-handed.

"And yet, you keep fighting. You're strong, I'll give you that. That's why it's going to be satisfying to kill you."

There's a loud *CLANG* as his sword makes contact with mine. Out of the corner of my eye, I see Drew and Nate wince at the echoing sounds of the swords. Gavin swipes the blade at my chest, but I quickly block it and try to strike him in the arm. He turns his body sideways and hacks the blade into my bicep.

"AH!" I scream, grabbing my skin as blood stains my fingers. I look down at my red hand and feel the pain for a few more seconds before the anger roars inside me, making me swipe at his body blindly.

"Try harder, Brooklyn!" Gavin mockingly calls, making a confident lunge at my leg. I step on the blade with one foot and kick him in the face with the other. Gavin roars in pain and watches blood from his broken nose drop onto the floor. He rips his sword from underneath my foot and tries to slice my other arm. I block his attack and start to push his blade away from me as they interlock. His face is a foot away from mine as we both try to force each other backwards. I put one of my feet behind the other so I can push harder. This is taking a toll on my injured arm which is holding the hilt. Gavin cruelly laughs.

"You're good," he snarls before he finally sends me reeling backwards with a final shove. I hit the wall on the other side of the room and let myself catch my breath as he stalks towards me. The lighting makes him look like a gaunt monster. "Unfortunately, it doesn't get you too far."

"I wouldn't say that," I breathe. Gavin comes at me and tries to catch me in the side. I duck underneath the blade, run past him, and cut him in the thigh on my way by. He whirls around, eyes lit with wrath, and we start to go at it, cutting and stabbing at whatever we can. I feel myself get hit in the arm again, my left leg, my right leg, and my ankle. I cut him a few times, but it's clear he's out for blood. Gavin's blinding rage has taken over his entire body. He's not in control anymore. Instead, a psychotic animal is pulling the strings. He's practically foaming at the mouth as he roars.

"YOU—" I get hit in the leg, "—DESERVE—" my left forearm gets slashed, "—TO—" my face takes a hit, "—DIE!"

The sword swiftly drives into the left side of my ribs.

I immediately let go of my sword and hit the ground, my eyes seeing white spots from the pain. Drew and Nate's muffled screams come from somewhere in the distance as I drop to the floor. My mouth gasps for air, and my hands desperately try to keep the blood inside of my body. It doesn't work. Too much blood is coming out. I'm trembling as I feel everything in my body slow down.

Gavin finally stops trying to murder me and watches as I lie on the concrete, blood gushing out of my side like water out of a hose. His sweaty hair hangs messily in his face. The spit and foam coming out of his mouth mixes with the sweat dripping off him nose and lands on the ground. Finally, his mouth twists into a terrifying smile, and he starts to laugh triumphantly.

"There we go," he hisses, coming over to me and watching as I writhe in pain. I'm crying as I roll onto my uninjured side, but I feel something in between my skin and the floor. That's when I remember the knife in my belt. They didn't take it away from me. I must've hidden it well. I slowly put one hand on the handle but keep the knife out of sight for the moment. Gavin doesn't seem too concerned with anything, besides gloating over my dying body.

"Congratulations. You're like your brother after all," I say in a quaking voice. "Go ahead." Gavin chuckles and puts his foot on my side, pressing down to make me scream.

"Oh, I'm going to drag this out for as long as possible. It's what you deserve." Gavin pushes harder on my body, and I shriek in pain. When I get the courage to open them up, the blurry outlines of Nate and Drew are looking at me in horror. Drew seems like she's crying too. Gavin takes his sword and puts it on my right cheek, turning my head so I'm forced to stare into his grey eyes that remind me so much of his brother's. Gavin clicks his tongue disapprovingly. "Look at Brooklyn Perce, lying on the dirt, where she belongs." He tilts his head to the side and crouches down. "And after all of that fighting, she's still a weak, scared, little child."

"You're going to regret this," I whisper, my grip on the knife tightening. Gavin clears the hair out of my face, inspecting it as though it was an antique.

"And why's that?"

"Witnesses," I say.

"Oh, I'm killing them after you," he says like it's obvious. Gavin's face contorts into a disturbing smile reminiscent of a clown's terrifying toothy grin. "Don't worry, Brooklyn. I learned from my brother. I'm never going to jail." His eyes light up like he has just thought of something exciting. "In fact, do you want to watch?" He goes to get up, but I grab onto his wrist with a decent amount of strength. There's a look in his eyes, like he's suddenly realized that something's not going as planned.

"I can't let you do that, Gavin," I muster. The grin slowly slides off his face, making way for fear and confusion, as I force the steak knife into his leg and use every last ounce of my strength to rip it downward towards his ankle. The screech that escapes his mouth is unlike anything I've ever heard. I've torn tendon, muscle, and probably chipped his bone.

Drew and Nate scream as they see blood flow forcibly out of Gavin. The madman grabs the hand I'm using to stab him, but I put my other hand on top of the knife so he can't take it out. I shove him away from me, and he staggers backwards, collapsing onto the floor. He's shrieking in agony but can't get up without the leg crumpling beneath him.

And so begins my journey of dragging my injured body across the grimy floor toward Nate and Drew, both of whom are looking at me with stunned expressions. Everything inside me is working overtime to make my way across the ground, the will to hang on for a few more seconds becoming the only thing sustaining me. When I get there, I feel like taking a break, but there's no time. My fingers deftly work on freeing Nate from the cable around his wrists and then pulling down his gag. Nate tries to untangle the cord holding his ankles together as I start to work on Drew, but before I can totally undo her cable, I grab onto my side and curl into a ball. A spastic pain runs through me, and I'm paralyzed on the ground for a second before yelping again. Gavin's high-pitched laugh rings throughout the cave as he watches me writhe in pain.

"Brook!" gasps Drew, the cloth out of her mouth. Her voice sounds like it's coming through a tube. "Nate, what's happening?" I feel someone put my upper half onto their lap. My mouth hangs open as I begin to lose control of my jaw. My head rolls back as Nate cradles me in his arms. Drew catches my head on its way toward the floor.

"Brooklyn?" Nate asks in a scratchy but urgent voice.

"Wha…," I answer weakly, looking at his blurred outline.

"Brook, it's okay. It's gonna be okay," Nate promises as he looks at me. Drew can't seem to bring herself to say anything.

"It … hurts," I whisper, though I can barely hear myself.

"I know. It's gonna be better soon," Nate tells me. Deciding it's too much work to stay open, my eyes shut for too long. Only when I force them to open again does Nate's panicked face come briefly into focus., causing Nate to panic more. His thumb wipes the tears off my cheeks. I've made it over to my friends, I've freed them, and the will to keep going has passed. An overwhelming desire for a hug from my mother washes over me, making me cry harder.

"I want my mom," I beg. "I want to see Mom." Nate's fuzzy form looks to Drew, who puts her head in her hands. "Nate, I don't … I don't wanna die," I plead with him. "I want my mom."

"I know, Brooklyn," Nate whispers, looking down at my side. "We're gonna get you out of here, you'll see your mom, I promise." He puts his hand on mine, the one covering my wound. Nate holds my other hand and puts it on his cheek. I feel large, hot tears rolling down his face. Things are becoming blurrier by the second, and a ringing sound in my ears is steadily growing in volume.

"I'm scared," I barely breathe.

"It'll be alright. We're gonna make you better, I promise. We're going to make you …" He trails off as I stop taking steady breaths. Drew starts to cry harder and clears the hair out of my face. The two of them look down on me as the moonlight from the ceiling grate becomes brighter and brighter.

"I'm… I'm…" I mouth as the light is blinding me. My eyes close on the blotchy image of Nate's beautiful face as his arms embrace me closely. He lets out a heart-shattering sob. With the sob comes Gavin's psychotic cackle. That's the last thing I hear before I feel my body shut down.

21

"Brooklyn!" It's Nate. We're on the roof of his freshman dorm as the sun rises. The colors in the sky are straight out of a painting. It's unlike anything I've ever seen. Blues, purples, oranges, yellows, and reds blend together to form a fantastic display. The entire city is laid out under our feet. The state of Nate's suit, with its undone tie, lets me know we've been up here for a while. He stands with his back to the sunrise and his arms outstretched. "What do you think?" He smiles his perfect smile as I look around and take it all in. It's all so quaint from up here, so quiet and calm.

"It's beautiful," I breathe. Nate walks towards me.

"You could see this every day if you wanted," he tells me. I look at him like he's kidding. "This could be all yours. You deserve this. After everything you've been through. You could be queen of this." I look out hungrily over the city. Every building beneath me, every tree and every person could become part of my home. "Take my hand and let's go." Nate stretches his hand out to me. There's an ominous feeling I get in my gut as I look at his palm.

"That's it?" I ask. Nate nods. The more I look at him, the more handsome he looks.

The more fake he looks.

"Don't think," Nate *says in a crueler tone than before. I look at his hand again.*

Then I start to remember ...

I look down at my stomach and see the red stain on my shirt, where the blood came through. When I look back at Nate, *his hand is within reach. He smiles at me.*

"C'mon, Brooklyn," he whispers. *I look from him to his hand and then realize where I am and the choice I'm being given. This can't possibly be it. It can't be over. As tempting as it would be to stay in this beautiful place forever, I take a step back.*

"No," I tell him.

The colors in the sky run and wash away, the sunny day is suddenly shrouded in clouds, and Nate *vanishes without a trace.*

^^^

I hear Darth Vader breathing.

In ... Out ... In ... Out ... In ...Out ...

No, that's me.

How am I not dead?

My eyes open for long enough to see the blank white ceiling and lighting of a hospital. Everything in the room is just oddly shaped blobs of different colors. Adjusting to the light takes some work. There's an oxygen mask over my nose and mouth. I feel numb all over. When I look to my left, I see the relieved faces of two people I know.

"Mom?" I'm not even sure if I say the right word. The woman makes a sound of joy.

"Hi, sweetheart," she whispers, smiling. I look to the man, tilting my head slightly. He looks like he's trying to keep it together with his hands shoved in his pockets and a thin smile on his face.

"Dad?" The man nods.

"Hello, Brooklyn," he says, trying to fight back tears. My mom squeezes my hand. I look around slowly, with my eyes half open.

"I'm so tired," I mumble.

"I know, sweetheart. But you're safe, it's alright now," says Mom lovingly.

"Safe …?"

Then, I vaguely remember dying in my boyfriend's arms.

"Nate." I'm completely sure I say *that* name correctly.

"He's okay. He's in another room," my mom reassures me. I let out a bigger breath, smile slightly, and then shut my eyes, letting my brain enter a drug-induced dreamless sleep.

^^^

When my eyes open again, I see Kenni's face, looking down at me. She lets out a sigh of relief when she sees me glance around the room.

It's the same room that I was in before, but it's decidedly less blurry. There's no mask over my face, either. There are windows to my left, with a door in the opposite left corner. A few vases of flowers sit on a side table to my right, next to the stand that holds my IV bag. Kenni looks like she hasn't slept in days as she stares at me, with a forced smile.

"Hey, Brook," Kenni whispers like she's talking to a wounded animal. I can't see myself, but by the way she's staring at me, I must look awful.

"Hey …" I keep trying to look around to get my bearings, but the doctors must have me on painkillers. I feel like my head weighs about a hundred pounds when

I try to move it even the slightest bit. Despite the large amount of opiates in my system, there's a sharp pain in my left side when I adjust myself even a little bit. Kenni glances at my ribcage and shakes her head.

"I wouldn't move if I were you," she advises. "The doctor told me if you stay still, you'll feel better."

"Why would I need to stay still?" I ask as I attempt to remember what happened to me before I was—

Stabbed.

All at once, I remember being pierced by a rough sword and falling on old stone below the church in the graveyard.

I glance down at my stomach and see the hospital gown I'm wearing is tinged with red above my rib cage. When I look back to Kenni, she shakes her head.

"How many stitches?" I ask.

"They told me, but I forgot the number. Enough to keep you together." I gulp as I gently lift my gown to see a massive white gauze pad below my left ribcage that's taped around my stomach. The pad goes around my back as well. I try to lift the gauze, but Kenni stops me. "Don't lift it. It might get infected. The doctors said they had to do a blood transfusion." I feel like I might vomit. I rest back into the pillows and squeeze my eyes shut, forcing myself to remember.

"Is anyone else in the hospital?" I ask her.

"Drew left yesterday. Issac was alright, and so was Brendon. Nicole is still here. She went the longest without any treatment, so her cuts might be infected, and she definitely lost weight while she was down there." Kenni smiles again. "Thank God you found them, Brook."

"Yeah ... Thank God," I agree, still out of it. Then a name jumps to my mind. "Where's Nate?"

As if in response to my question, there's a small knock on the door.

Kenni turns around in her seat, and we both glance towards the door as Nate slowly comes into the room holding flowers. Although he doesn't turn completely to me at first, I can see healing bruises decorating his jaw, arms, and forehead, and there's a certain raggedness in his eyes. Nevertheless, his lips make a weak smile.

"I'll let you get some rest then," she says like she's letting me in on a secret. "See you later, Brook. Feel better."

"Thanks, Kenni," I say in a scratchy voice. Kenni nods and then goes to the door. Nate holds it open for her and looks thankfully at her before letting the door shut behind her. He walks towards me with a small limp. Once Nate puts the flowers on my side table, I reach out my hand, and he takes it, sitting down next to me.

"Hey," he whispers. I put my hand on his face and bring him closer to me so I can kiss him. Nate kisses me softly like he's worried I may crack. When he breaks from me, I have to hold back tears.

"I-I had a nightmare," I stutter, swallowing and remembering the waxy version of him I encountered.

"It wasn't real," Nate says firmly with a little smile. "Whatever you saw, it was fake, no matter how real it felt." I nod, trying to calm myself down. "How are you feeling?"

"Out of it," I answer.

"I can imagine. You've been knocked out for two days," Nate tells me. I raise my eyebrows, suddenly feeling more awake than ever.

"*Two days*?"

"Brook, you lost a lot of blood."

"So I've been told," I say. "What about you?"

"They stitched up my leg, and I was allowed to leave yesterday. That's why I have this damn limp." Nate pauses. "Brook, I'm so sorry. About everything. I shouldn't have left you at the house that night. Conor jumped me before I even got to the bus stop."

"It's alright. I'm just happy you're okay. When you called …" I trail off when I decide I don't want to remember the chilling feeling and decide to reroute my thoughts instead. "I'm thankful you're alright."

"How much do you remember?"

"I remember fighting Gavin, and I remember him stabbing me. That's where it cuts out." He nods, saying nothing. "What?"

"You don't remember freeing me and Drew?" When he says it, I vaguely remember undoing cable wire around their wrists and ankles as I was bleeding out.

"No, I sort of remember that," I correct.

"Do you remember what you did to Gavin?" Nate prompts. While I shake my head, the vision of me stabbing him in the leg comes to mind.

"Yeah, I-I do," I realize, sounding surprised with myself. "I got him in the leg with the knife from my kitchen." I quickly look around my room as though Gavin's going to jump out from a closet and try to kill me again. "Where is he?"

"Handcuffed to a hospital bed about a floor down. I passed by his room to get here," Nate says. "The cops are watching him." He shakes his head in disbelief and gently tucks my hair behind my ear. "I can't believe you made it, Brook. When the nurses told me you were alive, I didn't believe them." Nate's looking at me like I'm a miracle, but there's a gnawing thought in the back of my mind.

"I wish I wasn't." I don't even want to vocalize it, so when I do, it's barely a whisper. Nate hears it anyway and becomes confused.

"What? Why the hell would you say that?"

"Every second that I'm living, someone wants to come after me," I whisper. "As long as I'm alive, they're still going to want to get me. Taylor said when he gets out, he's going to bury me alive." Nate swallows hard. "I should've just died and taken Gavin with me."

"Brook—" I can tell he's getting upset, but I plow on.

"Because not only is Taylor going to get me, but Gavin's going to be on my ass too. I'm always going to have a price on my head for solving that damn mystery and outing those boys. I'll never live it down—"

"Stop," Nate orders. He's looking at me with a stony face and seems like he's holding back tears. It's an off-putting look on him.

"You know it's true," I murmur, swallowing hard. "They'll never be happy as long as I'm living."

"No. It's not true." He sounds like he's saying it to convince himself. Slowly, carefully, his hands wrap around mine. "You have so much good left to do, Brook. And I know it's hard, but you have to try. There are so many people who love you and are still here thanks to you. You deserve to live in spite of everything you've been through. I don't know if anyone else would have the guts to go through it, but you did." I don't say anything. As always, he's right. The voice of reason and consistency in my life has rang true once again. "And in the meantime, take up fencing. Or maybe boxing." That makes me smile. Nate smiles along with me and kisses me lightly on the cheek. I take a deep breath and shut my eyes, savoring the feeling of being with him once again.

22

Two weeks later, I hear my mom call my name from the dining room. She sounds a bit frazzled, but I don't know why. She's just cooking dinner for me and her.

"Brooklyn, honey, could you help me set the table?" she asks. I poke my head out of the bathroom, holding onto the towel that's wrapped around me. My wet hair drips onto the floor as I yell back.

"Just got out of the shower! Be right there!" I feel a furry thing against my leg and realize that Harley has slipped into the bathroom with me. He makes himself comfortable on the warm bathmat and lets out a contented sound. I shut the door and look back at him. "You missed me in the ten minutes I was gone, huh?" I kneel to give him a few pets on the head, and his eyes drift shut sleepily.

Quickly, I dry off my body and put my hair up in a towel. I have to make sure not to move too fast, though. With some difficulty, I crouch and grab the box of gauze pads and medical tape from underneath the sink. Getting back up is even more of a challenge. I clutch the wound on my left side with my free hand as though that'll stop it from aching. When I finally straighten up, I let out a little whimper. Harley's eyes flick open, and he picks his head up to see why his owner is in pain.

"It's okay. I'm okay," I breathe, but I don't know if I'm trying to reassure myself or my dog. Either way, Harley doesn't buy it. He keeps watching me as I unwrap a gauze pad and carefully position it over the scabbing hole in my abdomen. My dog softly whines as he watches me rip little pieces of medical tape to affix the pad to my skin. I can't put any pressure on the wound, or I'll scream. The first few times I wrapped it myself, I realized this.

After my brief stay at the hospital, the police and my nurses thought it would be best if I went home and returned after the Thanksgiving holiday so I could properly heal. I've been going crazy, staying in my house, nursing a wound that has been slow to heal. I've only seen Nate, Drew, Kenni, and Finn via video call and nothing else. I've gone outside, but I can't do much more than walk slowly around the neighborhood.

"Got it," I whisper triumphantly as I put the last bit of tape on my skin. When I finally straighten up and look at myself in the mirror, I feel the sudden urge to cry. Everything about my reflection is wrong. I should be smiling, not frowning. I should be able to stand up straight, but I can't, and my eyes should be glimmering, but the light in them has gone out. I'm incredibly tired. Nightmares and flashbacks have been keeping me up at night, and I don't have Nate to lull me back to sleep. Harley seems to have noticed this void in my life, but as much as he tries to make me feel safe by cuddling next to me, he could never understand what's going on in my head. That's why he's been more protective of me than usual. I'm convinced he can tell I'm in distress.

When I put on the rest of my clothes, I see that my phone is buzzing. Normally, I wouldn't pick up the phone, but when I see it's Nate calling, I can't refuse. I tap the screen and put the phone to my ear.

"Hey," I say, a little smile making its way onto my face.

"Hey. How are you?" What a loaded question nowadays.

"I'm doing well." It's not totally a lie.

"How's the pain today?"

"Better than yesterday, but only by a bit. What about you? What are you doing today?"

"I'm on my way home from my grandmother's. We had Thanksgiving dinner at her place. When I get home, I'm going into a food coma," Nate says. We both laugh a little, then the line is silent again. "What about you?"

"It's just Ma and me." I hear Harley whimper from his spot on the floor. After smiling, I add, "and Harley."

"Where's your dad?" Nate asks.

"Probably out with his friends at a bar somewhere, watching football," I say. "He didn't call, but why would he?"

"Because you're his daughter." There's silence on the line. I can tell Nate is trying to hold back anger. "Are you doing okay? Still having nightmares?"

"Yeah. Yeah, a lot of them," I grimace. "I'm so incredibly tired. You should see the bags underneath my eyes."

"I'm sure you still look beautiful with them," Nate comforts me. I smile at the tile floor. "When are you going back up to school?"

"Probably on Saturday. Mom's being extra cautious, though. She might have me stay home through the end of the semester."

"How would you do finals?"

"Most of them are papers, and the few tests I have I'd ask to take online." Harley gets up as I leave the bathroom. He follows me into my room and resumes his position on the floor.

"So, there's no chance I could see you before then?" I shake my head as if he can see it.

"I don't think so. I'd love to give you a hug, though. It might help me sleep," I say, truthfully. Nate laughs.

"I'd love to hug you too."

"Brook! Someone's at the door!" Mom calls from the dining room. "Can you get it, please?"

"Coming!" I yell. "Hold on one second." I put my phone to my chest, so he can't hear anything. I then run down the hall and through the living room to answer the door.

Standing outside of my house is my boyfriend dressed in khakis, a blue dress shirt, and brown shoes. His amber eyes and his lips are smiling at me.

"Hey, Brook," he says.

I drop my phone onto the carpet and fling myself into his arms, giving him the tightest hug that I can. He squeezes me and rests his head on top of mine. The hole in my side screams at me to release him, but I push past the pain and let myself sink into my boyfriend. Tears are running down my face, and I don't know if it's because of him or the pain. Nate kisses me on my forehead and looks at my puffy eyes.

"I knew it. You do look beautiful," he says, wiping away my tears. I laugh a little, and he does too. I hear my mom coming around the corner from the kitchen and turn around to look at her. "Hey, Ms. Perce."

"Nate! The drive up was okay?" she asks. I smile to myself.

"You knew about this?" I ask her.

"Honey, I coordinated it," she says. I leave Nate's arms to hug my mom.

"Thank you," I whisper to her. Harley has come into the room and happily trots up to Nate, mouth open, tongue out. My boyfriend kneels to pet my dog, who automatically rolls over, gratefully taking every stroke Nate's giving him.

"Are we ready to sit?" my mom asks when she's done hugging me.

"My hair's still wet," I say.

"The food will still taste amazing," Nate responds, coming up beside me to hold my hand. "Let's sit." I squeeze his palm and lead him into the dining room. We sit on the same side of the table, with my mom across from me. Harley nudges aside the seat opposite Nate, poking his nose up onto the table to smell the array of food my mom has laid out. A full turkey, stuffed with homemade stuffing, sits in the center, surrounded by a gravy boat, a small plate of canned cranberry sauce, a bowl of string beans with butter and spices, a vat of mashed potatoes, and a basket of rolls that look like they were just taken out of the oven. It's a small spread, but it's just enough for three people and a hungry dog. My mom reaches across the table to take my hand, her other hand resting on top of Harley's paw. I hold Nate's hand, and Nate follows my mom's lead with Harley's other paw.

"Nate, do you want to say grace?" my mom asks. Nate shakes his head.

"It's your home. You should do the honors," he says respectfully. Ma looks at me. I give her a look telling her to go for it. She takes a deep breath.

"Alright, let's see. We give thanks for the food on our table, the family and friends in our lives, and our health. We're grateful for everything being calm and having the chance to spend time with those we love." Once my mom decides that's enough, we let go of each other and start to dig into the food and for a moment, I forget all about school and the fraternity and Gavin. I leave behind all animosity and tiredness, letting myself live in the moment, this little moment, when I have the two people and the one animal that I love the most in one room. Tonight, I'll have nightmares, but for now, I'll take comfort in the waking moment.

THE END